Sangfroid

Sangfroid

MIA COLLINS

Library of Congress Control Number:		2022903984
ISBN:	Hardcover	978-1-6641-1737-2
	Softcover	978-1-6641-1736-5
	eBook	978-1-6641-1735-8

Print information available on the last page.

Rev. date: 03/01/2022

To order additional copies of this book, contact:
Xlibris
UK TFN: 0800 0148620 (Toll Free inside the UK)
UK Local: (02) 0369 56328 (+44 20 3695 6328 from outside the UK)
www.Xlibrispublishing.co.uk
Orders@Xlibrispublishing.co.uk
840446

SYNOPSIS

It wasn't nostalgia Tabitha was experiencing, but something more sinister. She had been walking around with her first Tattoo on her back put there by Jonny 31 years ago, they used to swim in the river together, splashing around, he would always freak out if a fish touched his leg or he couldn't touch the bottom, "put your feet down, the Islands just there, she would have to guide him and then burst out laughing". He would almost be having a panic attack, but Tabitha just found him hilarious, then he moaned too much about how the water was cold. It appeared her memories were wiped as far back as since she was a teenager, they weren't just faded but completely gone, he tried many times to make her remember him but he was a stranger to her all over again, for all the years they made memories, they'd just vanished, nothing could jog her mind, as far as she was concerned he was a stranger again every time they met. - Until one day her memories started to come back, she had this memory of a man's face who she clearly spent a lot of time with over the years but who was he? She would just brush it aside but then the others she'd forgotten too surfaced to her mind. Strangers from the past began to come in numbers and began to fill the missing jigsaw pieces, notifying her that Bea had bragged she was poisoning Tabitha's dogs by throwing rat poison over her garden wall, Bea exhibited alarming signs of mental illness, she showed no empathy or care for animals, what is she really capable of next. After Tabitha's attack she spent 2 weeks in a coma. Being spiked almost killed her. She was given CPR, with scarring left on her heart, the only thing she could recollect was being called in for a CT scan, to be told by a Dr she had amnesia. She had no recall of how her head injury occurred or to the extent it stretched and how it would affect her life from there on. The unknowing.- So her memories were coming back, what will she do with this knowledge, what happens next? All she knew was Jonny was the only person who could help her. But he's unlikely to ever do that, she doesn't want to drag him into her nightmare, so she needs to fight this alone. He has his life and she has hers.

CONTENTS

CHAPTER ONE

Tabitha was Born in Oxfordshire, England, although her family were from Ireland. Her grandparents moved to England during the war looking for work, as they were poverty stricken farmers, therefore needed to find a suitable future for their children and rapidly growing family, as the Irish do.

Mr and Mrs O'Dwyer, Jack being 7 years senior to Mary, was a hard working, a Head Cowman when they arrived in England. They'd left behind a home and land they loved, which is all they'd ever known as home, as teenage sweethearts.

The hardship of Mary losing her first born child Michael as a baby, to a house everyone in the village said was cursed that no child would be born to this house, they shrugged it off but once that happened they planned on saving up to leave, the plan was to emigrate to Canada, England being a stop off. By the time they had left Ireland with the infamous funny memories of Mary being the talk of the village by being a funny tiny 5 ft tall 6stone

Young woman who was the only person to hop on a cow facing backwards then ride it across a field just because she had that mischiful streak in her.

When Mary was 12 she went missing from her Ballylanders home, (Tanners field) set off across the fields by passing the bogs, she was wise to the land and where not to step. This one particular sunny morning she got it into her mind to go on a long adventure. She walked all day and didn't return home until past 12 midnight. Her Parents fuming, worried sick, gave her a good telling off on her late return.

She said she had it in her mind to go to the top of the Galtee mountain, to which she accomplished with pride and exhaustion. She had a very close relationship to her father whom she loved dearly, also a sister and 4 brothers, 2 from her fathers first marriage as he was a widow, she didn't see them again after they left for war. Mary's favourite brother Topper due to his fierce war stories, whom she sadly lost touch with when she left for England with 2 children Pat and Peggy.

Now Jack used to deliver the churns of milk around the villages from the farm. He owned

a little cart along with 2 shire horses to pull him everywhere he needed to be.

Mary owned a racing horse, with long sleek legs built for speed which she would often gallop at full speed even jumping the hedges as a shortcut to where she was going or just for fun, Mary rode bareback most of the time as she told her stories.

Mary used to work as a maid in a Large stately home for a wealthy man who fell in love with her. He left the house along with the land to her but due to the curse she believed in, Mary left it behind to go to ruins. So you understand the background, they fell in love, they got married, had 4 boys and 4 girls. Upon Raising these children in England, they moved around a lot, Little Faring being the first tied cottage with a farm job Jack proudly landed himself on his feet, but the house wasn't in great condition for their rapidly growing family. It had one large bedroom so wasn't suitable to stay for long. The O'Dwyer family moved to a village in the countryside called Ballycot in Oxfordshire, they lived in around 7 of the local houses until they finally settled into the one that had running water and a bath with the luxury of electricity, because the ones all before that had a water pump in the garden,those were very hard times, the bath was a tin tub they'd need to boil the kettle over the rayburn to heat up the water. So this house was a luxury to what they had been used to struggling with.

Mary said the Irish sea with the horse and carriage ride across Ireland was a jouncy, bone shaking,unbearably awful, and exhausting for them with the small children being toddlers at the time, and Mary pregnant with baby Jack. Their plan and dream to go live in Canada had crumbled due to Mary falling pregnant again. This is detrimental to their ability to ever save the money for the rest of their trip. Not only that the long travels had put Mary off even attempting to go that far ever again, sadly she decided to give up on her dreams for the sake of the children needing a stable home. Mary just wanted to settle down in front of a cosy open fire at the end of each hard working day to relax with her crochet and have her babies wrapped up warm in their beds with the one toy they owned each. They were poor so one toy was all they could afford, doesn't that put a perspective on today's times.

Mary and Jack, after their own children had grown and flown the nest, weren't planning on another child to raise but then came Tabitha.. her mother being incarcerated into a mental facility by the time she turned 4. Tabitha sat watching the men in white coats drag her violently from the house after her breakdown, throwing items into the street below, one of said items was a picture of Jesus, as it glided down landing point blank over the Policeman's head breaking the glass but the frame went around his shoulders. This picture itself still stands reframed of course to this day in the family home. I guess the Policeman was the laughing stock of the situation for a long time thereafter. Bernadette O'dwyer spent a year or two in a facility but was never the same coming out. Tabitha had gotten used to the fact she wasn't all there mentally, therefore had to suck it up and teach myself how to do things. Most people learn more after school, she learned more in school from friends as the parental talks never come about in that house being a strict catholic home certain things weren't allowed to be discussed.

A cold bike ride two miles to church every sunday morning until Tabitha's grandparents were too old to make the journey any longer, then Sundays became about relaxing, gardening or a good old black and white movie on the tiny portable tv, this was the area the child was the tv remote, if you understand that you lived through the 70s and 80s. They used the excuse that they couldn't find the channels as fast as she could.

So Tabitha's upbringing is that of mixing with a large family every weekend. Her uncles and aunts would visit us with her cousins all older than herself. She was the baby for a short time anyway. There would be the men in the kitchen playing darts, the women would have already cooked the roast for the day and washed up.. They would be scattered around the house doing odd jobs for my grandparents tidying the beds or dusting off the mantlepiece, they didn't sit still often always looking for something to do, if it wasn't swapping the curtains over for a fresh pair or bringing down gifts of some sort it was a very supportive family. Lots of loud laughter and smoke filled air, Tabitha hated the smoke she found it hard to breath when they all sat smoking around her, infact it was clear offput to her when she grew up she never took to fags at all.

Jack on his retirement had his large garden at the back filled with every vegetable, fruit you name it he had it, and I mean a meticulous line of veg to a high standard no chemicals used just a constant daily hobby he did to get out the house come rain or shine. Tabitha would often hear her grandmother shout" if you don't come in for your dinner it's going in the dog or your tea going down the drain and you'll miss out." but Jack didn't take a rest until the day he died. He loved his gardening with a passion. In the front garden he had fastidiously shaped pretty little hedges, evergreens over hung the side path, he grew his flowers all round all colours people would visit the village. You would often see tourists taking photos of the front of the house and the display of pretty plants he had growing over the gateway. Jack was a very strict man laying down the law when needed but a quiet man combined with being a gentleman, Jack treated his wife respectfully but when it came to disrespecting men he was known to have a clean knock out punch, his advantage having very large hands and fierce temper if crossed. He told Tabitha a story of a donkey that kicked him one time and he punched it in temper and the poor thing went down to the ground. He said he regretted it immediately as he loved animals but it caught him off guard as a quick tempered reflex. John also later had his son Pat working on the farm for a couple years working for a man called Hender, who lived in the manor house at Ballycot, in Henders will he said when he dies he wants Jack O'Dwyer to live in that tied cottage until his death, hence a 99 year lease was drawn up in the will, but the house was left to the National Trust, but Jack lived his days renting it from them.

When Jack was middle aged he was working fixing the fence in a field with a large bull, he knew the risks but this day he let his guard down, the bull came charging at him launching Jack into the air breaking his leg, as he landed inside the field. Pat, Jacks son witnessed this he ran quickly jumped over the fence to where Jack lay, shouting waving at the bull to get it away from his dad but it didn't work the bull flipped Jack one more time, this time he landed the other side of the fence to safety, with relief at that moment Pat jumped back over to go tend and get help for his dad laying on the ground in agony.

During the weeks of recovery which ended up happening twice in fact, as a tree Jack was felling landing on both his legs breaking them simultaneously, on this occasion landed him up to rest again.

So Mary would often sit in her retirement from the hotel, by listening to her Irish Rebel songs on her grand gramophone, Mary would often antagonize the English neighbors but being a rebel and a dark sense of humor would just turn it up even more. She had her fair share of descrimiation which led to this later cantankerous behavior in life but being a little old lady she got away with it often. I would say that they were proud to back down and too proud to lower their standards from anything but the way of the catholic church. Being a girl growing up in this old fashioned household had Tabith rebelling as a teenager. At age 14 Tabitha had myself a job in the local pub working behind the scenes not serving the bar of course. But socially she soon learned mixing with older peers was a more pleasant and mature life than that of some her own age who seemed immature.

CHAPTER TWO

Now Tabitha, her childhood was wrapped up in cotton wool, spoilt although poor upbringing her family surrounding her were very protective being a large family she had older cousins to go sort anything out that needed to be done, you could say a form of protection that led into adulthood of the men being feared to not being a family to be tampered with. Eventually everybody grew up therefore said behaviour settled down married but not before raising the roof in their youth first.

She strongly believed in the religion she was raised with, although a rebelling teen she soon settled into her own motherhood having six children herself. Not without breaking a few hearts along the way. Tabitha was not the sort to be emotional or heartfelt. Not until later on in age of course she was known to be ruthless and not hold onto heartstrings before she was off again looking for something else to keep herself occupied, men would come and go in her life she wasn't one to settle down, well she didn't want to for a very long time anyway.

Tabitha at the age of Ten had learnt herself to swim in the weir at Ballycot, nobody to watch her at this age she had to rely on faith and luck her childhood was adventurous, wild and fun. She would swim across the rapid waterfall waves lashing towards her. She became a very strong swimmer within days of learning, Tabitha was an extremely fit child, athletic and that carried on into her late 30s," it's all downhill from 30 her grandmother used to say."

The surrounding village was picturesque. Visitors from all over the country come to visit this beautiful countryside. During the summer months the field would be packed with sunbathers, rubber dinghies, lilos and blown up tractor inner tubes. The river was swarming with people trying to cool in the water, splashing, laughing, rope swings from trees, and high dive bank dares into the deepest parts if you were brave enough. The swans, the ducks would go sit on the bank out the way during this chaos of the day and be settled back by the late afternoon fishing for their dinner. Of course in the winter months there were almost as many fishermen sitting around the banks until the license man came along to check if you had one, sometimes you'd see a quick exit or a good excuse given by the youths. Along the river there were some old gun houses built during the war. So it has some history as well as beauty, including the fountain in the center of the village which used to be the maid water source for the village before they installed taps in the houses. This tap can still be used for drinking water today. It has four corner seats placed nicely around it with steps going down on all four sides it had a nice tiled roof with beautiful beams built to not only look good but to last a lifetime. The family house being right next to it meant Tabitha often used the tap to wash her cars or motorbikes she owned throughout the years. During the summer months the children would often entertain themselves playing marbles there or just having a good old fashioned water fight.

Growing up there were 12 children in the village Tabitha knew them all. From the antics of skating across ponds in winter or the river if it overflowed into fields, the locals would be up to dangerous sports but lucky no fatalities. Teresa was a slight tom boy as a child climbing trees, building her own bikes, to dangerous stunts jumping her bikes and doing tricks. She wasn't really aware of herself until she was 15 even then not quite aware of what she had going for her own self confidence was very low in a girli respect.

_She never abandons her spirit of artlessness or naivete.

One sunny afternoon Tabitha was in her front garden when a young man came running past her gate with long dark hair frantically asking her to hide him. "Quick quick he insisted,"help me hide, this was Hollywood star who was living secretly in a close by location, so she hastily made a choice as they ran together down the path to the car park at the end of the village Tabitha swifty jumped into the hedge across a deep dried up ditch where Jonny Stepp followed, sitting next to her thanking her he placed his hand on the middle of her back. She turned to the right to face him as she did so he kissed her on the right corner of her mouth, which was almost her first kiss. He said I like you, shall we make out,in a faint American accent? Tabitha turned to look at him in astonishment. The most ridiculous thing she could have ever said was" I'm a virgin! '' At this point his eyes widened with surprise "oh …..then you better go away and get some experience first" sorry. Which was a relief as she hadn't even had her first crush by this time she was still more interested in hanging out with her friends than men. Before she could think of anything more to say they were found by the group he was hiding from, guessing it maybe was his friends they were very angry at him for running off. At this point Tabitha took it upon herself to sneak away home. She didn't know that this moment would vanish from her memory for the next 34 years. - ?...........

A couple years went by and she began to bump into this man on the odd occasion, one day he called her over outside a shop after chatting shortly Jonny said "you can go",Tabitha said who'd you think you are the king of England she thought he was arrogant and put him in his place..anyway nothing deeply serious but they had enough encounters to know each other intimately over the years that came ahead but not a commitment. He sent Huge bunches of flowers a few times even asking her out on an official date. She turned him down on some occasions but gave in when she was 17. He sent a car to her to collect her and bring her to him, the date was cut short and the driver took her home again. This didn't come to anything. They would often bump into each other in towns, he would hop in her car go for a quick joy ride round, they hung out chatted laughed a lot become friends and just got on with their own lives, but fate kept bringing them to the same places right up into her late 30s they'd still have this connection of attraction where he would approach her for more than friendship, often if they had both been partying drinking they'd end up at one another's houses for the night. But the next day would be brushed off and moved on forgotten about.

As the years went on Tabitha forgot who he was. - "Completely"! His memory totally wiped from her mind, she would often bump into him 100s of times over the years and yet each time she saw him he was a stranger again. He tried to take her and stand in the spot they kissed on new years eve, he tried to remind her by telling her little things about their nights together, but nothing, absolutely no memory of the man he had become a total stranger to her all over again.

CHAPTER THREE

FLASH BACKS

Tabitha recently turned 47. Looking back at her life she had her ups and downs, but nothing like this. She began to experience PTSD, but not in a panicky way. She wasn't sure at first what it was as she hadn't experienced anything like it before but reading up on it and common sense it soon accrued to her she was experiencing a mild form of this due to the amount of involuntary memories coming back to her. Nothing that stopped her carrying on with her daily life was just an annoying raindrop of memory that at first made no sense, but after two half years it became apparent these were like jigsaw pieces that all fitted together into a one long 26 year period of lost memories that were now coming to surface. It wasn't just memories, it was new memories holding onto knowing people, this man wasn't the only man she had forgotten but the only one who seemed to be slightly aware of her memory loss by the fact he was the only person to try and remind her each time they- re-met !

How could she possibly try to tell people what she was experiencing? The doctors seemed too lazy to look up medical files, so Tabitha had to do all her own research.

So time went on, the flash backs came daily for two and half years not solid just a trickle here or there when she wasn't trying to think about it, there it would be a memory would flow like watching a reel on a film from the past she could see what they were wearing as if she was in the room again, feel and remember word for word spoken in those moments. Knowing a 100% it was real she tried to tell others but people would gaslight her at first, until she finally found old friends she lost touch with in the early years who told her he was there he remembers the things she recalls to be real memories as he remembers the same thing. That was reassuring, as for those who chose to keep a secret from her not helping her remember she would deal with them later in a way that says abandon them as friends who need friends that try to lie and cover up this strange thing that's been happening to her, -a big secret hidden from her selfishy by others.

So this man, came in and out her life in the randomest places they'd bump into each other, he give her her first tattoo, she went to him not realising he was in that shop he'd hung out there in his younger days to take up the hobby in his spare time not a job just in between his working away. She even bumped into him in LA while on her honeymoon, he spoke to her across the road and shouted "Tabitha do you want me to show you around? "Perplexed" She waved her wedding ring as she hadn't a clue who he was again, said sorry im married smiled and went back to her Motel as she was previously wandering around Hollywood on foot exploring her surroundings and almost getting lost, then soon realised she should have stayed indoors as not many people seemed to do that in America, but she loved to walk.

Tabitha couldn't hold onto a single memory of ever being with Jonny Stepp each and every time they met in later years as the first ten years he was known to her, after that gone wiped. Nothing familiar, nothing whatsoever.

It was so strange to experience this kind of loss but also her own family had been lying to her about things to pursue her into things against her will by manipulation and just plain violence. You see Tabitha fell pregnant by this man not once but twice, he thought three times he was convinced her first child was his after seeing her pregnant one day after a fling six months before. The two had these flings, moments, nights spent with each other where she had fallen pregnant during the time the memory loss was so bad she had no recollection of sleeping with him, he would come to her house with flowers and try to tell her but she thought he was making it up she was convinced she didn't know him a man she met as a child trick or treating at his house to the moment in the hedge, to the moments of driving round together over the years. Making out in unusual places, roof tops, against walls, grass banks, even in the trunk of a car where she fell pregnant that night. In graveyards to inside his house upon the stairs in a cinema room and in his bed on another occasion where she slept alone as she upset him that evening. All these moments lost then suddenly back too late when he's got on with his life now and she's there trying to figure out what any of it means or why is it back- why didn't it stay lost - What use is it now?

Flash backs.......

So it's new years eve back when she was in her early 20s, she's in a bar Jonnys standing on the other side of the bar he keeps peeking back over to her. She doesnt recognise him - The bar man says 'last orders' and shouts for her to leave the bar. It's 11pm, she replies it's new years eve.-" What am I supposed to do for a hr?" It's cold and all the other bars are locked. Jonny says to the bar man to let her stay. So he starts to send over drinks, paying for them for the rest of the evening, she thanks him shyly. He's flirting by pretending to copy her body language, making her laugh, this goes on a while. She has to walk past him to the ladies, he grabs her arm as he does so slides it down to her hand pulling her back as she passes him, he says "hi" are you going to come and talk to me, Tabitha replies;" yes in a moment ", and carries on to the ladies. On return she hasn't a clue what to say to him so walks past nervously, he again grabs her arm, "come talk to me," she pulls away smiles and says in a minute, but walks back to her corner to just be shy.

Almost 12midnight everyone begins to walk to the town square, she's standing outside Barclays bank next to the curb. Another man who was also chatting to her in the bar a caterer was near her,- the town was alive with cheers and excitement, the celebrations were at a all time high, people were beginning to pear off right before the countdown .....10-9-8......7-6...Tabitha felt awkward she could see the long haired man standing against the bank wall looking at her through the crowd like he'd not taken his eyes off of her.. She turned to leave thinking this isn't for her after all something felt wrong she felt it was time to just go right now before the 1 had been counted. Suddenly as she went to leave she was whisked around then a kiss planted on her, champagne, the rain and cheers,with flashes of a camera in their faces.

This kiss seemed to linger, both enjoying the moment and unwilling to pull away, not that she minded he was a good kisser. After it eventually came to an end he asked "will you come have a champagne bath with me?" -she thought, she'll never see him again so it won't happen therefore she said yes, he replied Yes with excitement .. so there she was thinking what have I just agreed to now? The next minute he's said something to his friend who's grabbed Tabitha by the arm as she's rushed into the back alley into a hotel apartment.

Half hr before she overheard him saying to his friend in the bar "I'll pay you £250 pound to keep Kath busy for 10 min. I just need ten min please man.." His friend said no, it's new years eve no, he then replied £2500 that's the best offer you're gonna get to do this for me ? So.. he agreed, at this point he leaned over the bar ordering £750 worth of champagne, Tabitha wondered what on earth he needed that for then it occurred to her after the request about the bath.. Ahh, the penny dropped.

Tabitha was told to go into the bedroom and wait but she fell asleep due to the amount of drinks he had sent to her over the bar earlier that evening. She sensed someone laying on the bed next to her, he's laying there posing for a photo while she sleeps and his Kath on the other side of her both in a fit of giggles.

Tabitha wakes slightly, seeing him goes to grab him in a daze but he leaves the room, she gets up to go to the loo as he said so are we doing this or what? She wanders off to the bathroom and pulls the plug as she's already forgotten his plans. It was cold and sticky anyway. It would have been awful in that cold hotel room. So she let £750 worth of champagne go down the plug hole. A week later a gigantic basket of flowers arrives for her and he appears at her gate, oh well that's good she won't be after money looking at her house from the outside.. The gate is between them, he asks "are you Tabitha?" -"Yes" in her reply she's confused and dubious, he points both hands to his chest then to his car where he has a driver "would you like to come out on a date with me ?" she thinks quickly as shes not really had time to consider this question so goes with no sorry I have a boyfriend, he replied what' what about new years eve the kiss ? Tabitha didn't remember the kiss, or maybe a fragment of it but she didn't realise it was him. He turned afoot then shouted `` you win some you lose some ", running to the car shouting drive and they headed off towards the river which was a dead end. They turned the car around as she walked and stood under the fountain on the steps, the car pulls up he gets out hands her his card it has a local number on it and says, if you change your mind this is my card, at that moment a man hops out the American car and the same big flash camera from new years eve flashes a few photos of them together. He gets in the car again and they drive off. Going back inside the flowers read- "Sorry"! The plain white card printed a local number as where she lived, with the name Johnny Stepp. And his business details.

So Tabitha is a teenager, possibly 17 or thereabouts, she's going for a walk in the village where she lived, out pops Jonny from nowhere, she jumps in surprise, didn't expect to see him there in a graveyard she always took a shortcut through. So he ran into the house next door, a mansion, it contained a boat house under it at that period, and its own cinema. So he grabbed a load of beers, jumped back over the wall and rejoined her. They sit in the hot sunshine of the peaceful warm afternoon chatting and laughing for hrs. They walk around he's very touchy feely holding hands facing her tryin to come close while she's keeping him at arm's length unsure if it's worth ruining a bonding moment to take it too far.

Then he becomes brash and says i'm going to shag you, it's definitely going to happen and laughs with confidence she replies no you're not laughing back at him. Unsure if he meant it the drink was kicking in and the hot sun was pounding down. Before she knew she's laying on her back looking up at him laying over the top of her how did she get to this moment, lust was all it was, the next min they're laying in the grass under a tree the other side of the graveyard he's gone and got a camera he's taking photos of her telling her to undress, she undoes two buttons, he then rips her white blouse open destroying the remaining buttons grabs the camera and records her reaction which was 'you idiot why did you do that,' he said i told you to show more laughing, she was mad about the blouse not so much about the moment they were about to get into. He's laying on top of her kissing her neck and almost down to her breast, at this five min later they are naked under the tree. Suddenly a man walks past and catches them. Jonny jumps up, runs in circles shouting..." shit shit shit," holding his pants up and trousers around his ankles and falls over. Tabitha is trying to grab her clothes to get dressed but she can't stop laughing hysterically at him because of the fact they've been caught. The man leaves after promising to not say a word about this, Jonny then runs back to Tabitha grabs her hand then they run frantically climbing over the wall and run into the house. They run around upstairs in several rooms and finally end up on the stairs with the large front door wide open as the heat of the moment is brought to an end with his satisfaction being granted. He was so intense like he had a desire to take what he wanted passionately. He suddenly changes his tune, Tabitha is swiftly thrown back over the wall, he was only using her for pleasure. So her journey home was treacherous in the state she was in from drinking all afternoon in the hot sun. The moment was forgotten about immediately. She was exactly the same minded she could equally use a man for pleasure and not be emotionally tied.

The years went by again, she was out drinking in a local bar, Jonny's there he's also trying all night to flirt with her, grabs her outside toward the end of the evening, "Tabitha, "you like me don't you?" I mean you like me as man do you tell me you like me Tabitha?" She's unsure as she was enjoying being single at this stage, not quite sure what she wanted or was even looking for but he then suddenly grabbed round the waist and began to kiss her neck....he knew it was her achilles heel, he took her by the hand led her to the spot he kissed her new years eve years before, trying to remind her, stood her on the spot, said look up at me i'm standing on the curb you were stood down the step, remember me please.. He pleaded, he grabbed her shoulders, turned her around, said look, imagine the crowns cheering, imagine this spot remember this remember us kissing !! Sadly there were no memories she had nothing as far as she was aware he was a stranger..

He walked her back to the bench where he told her thinks he made her pregnant a couple years before, she said no we haven't met, he went on to explain how he'd come home with her to her home stayed the night she has examined every inch of tattoos all over his body, he told her he had given her her first tattoo, he explained the night they spent together how he enjoyed it for her to tell him to leave upon awakening because she didn't know who he was again in the morning.. This clearly upset him, tears in his eyes as he left. So he starts to say in the present sitting on the bench I want to show you my bedroom and smirks, she laughs and repeats that you want to show me your bedroom really. I heard that one before and laughs. So they begin to walk the main road but he's volatile as his moods begin to swing. She says well I think it's too far to walk in heels....... So turns and falls in the grass on the side of the road, he reaches down both arms to help her up and he falls on top of her. For a moment their eyes meet, suddenly he's all over her frantically undoing her blouse, lifting her skirt. The heat of the moment made them forget where they were again.

They walk back to the bar where there's a crowd of men outside laughing. Look at the state of that bird she's got grass in her hair and her buttons are all done up wonky.. He was also covered in grass, no denying what had just happened.

So they start to walk home to a friends place to stay over as she couldn't get a cab, as she's walking she grabs Jonny's arm, and his friends arm walking slightly merry they do a funny walk the three of them leg over leg, shocked they didn't end up in a heap.. She turns to his friend, asks his name, he says Ryan Goose, she mocks it, asks what do you do he said I like to take photos, I'll take some of you when we get back if you like, she replied I'm not photogenic. And i'm not coming home with you two strange men, then Jonny shouts pointing his arm at her you're the girl from Ballycot? - like the penny had just dropped he knew her from their younger days but years had gone by.

They say their goodbyes and tabitha goes into a mates house. She's asleep immediately, it being so late. She's laying on the sofa wearing just a white sheet, she hears her name shouted several times outside, its Jonny banging on the door demanding her number from her mate he's told to go away, but he's fighting for her he won't give up, she walks to the door he grabs her pulling her outside with him but shes still naked, no time to grab anything but this sheet because he's just spent a hr shouting for her to come outside to come to him, he passses her a bottle of whisky, as he does so, the sheet drops, it's the middle of the night so it's dark and nobody can see except him. He stands frozen for a moment then bends down grabs the sheet and ties it around her covering her modesty, but then he drags her by the hand, runs with her round the corner and takes her against the wall in the heat of passion. A car drives past stops and takes photos but they don't stop or care if it just felt right.

They begin to walk the miles and miles trip to his place on foot barefoot and in pain her feet bleeding from the long hard road. They talk, they walk, they stop along the way again the heat of the moment kept happening all the way home, he said, when a car passes I keep catching a glimpse of your naked body and its making me horny and this he jumps onto the grass verge lays back and demands she show him what she can do....shortly after this heat of passion again, -she collapsed unconscious. In a panic he flags down a car, they lift Tabitha into the boot and Jonny climbs in next to her, lays down and holds her in his arms while she sleeps. She wakes inside the pitch black car trunk, she can see the tail light giving out a slight light to his cowboy hat she had been calling him cowboy all night and he was snapping. It was not a cowboy hat which to her was funny to wind him up so she kept saying it even more.

So she's in the boot, he's laying on the left . He starts to touch her, starting down her leg and sliding his hand upwards this awoke her, he asks "did I just make you pregnant in the grass, or can I make you pregnant, will you have my baby..?" Fuck it he said and hes kissing her and slides himself into her, so this is happening in a car boot the most strange heat of the moment place appart from the roof of the villae hall they had been years before, or the graveyard which she couldnt remember at this precise time. -Still a blank of memory absolutely she really had forgot him.

CHAPTER FOUR

After they arrive back to Jonny's place his friends are there waiting, Tabitha is unable to stand by this point the sheet was falling off her along the road and a car had stopped reversed, snapping a photo of her naked holding his hand as they walked.

His friend comes out and carries her as he lifts her the sheet falls away and all is seen the laughter of his friends. She's too drunk to care at this stage. Inhibitions gone. She's placed upright and handed a drink in the living room by Kath Myer, at this point she is sick all over a Kaths shoes, then collapses luckily one of the men caught her carrying her and places her in the bath. She wakes up with Jonny sitting over her washing her sore feet and mud from her body. She looked up and he said -"you're beautiful !" she replied you're quite cute, but she can't stay awake and passes out.

The two men Ryan Goose and Pete Decor ..

Tabitha Had drunk most of the bottle of whisky Jonny handed to her while walking along the road barefoot, it seemed to help take her mind off the pain. She hopped onto the grass bank in some parts of the walk. The grass was softer to her sore feet than the road but it made her feet filthy.

The deep sleep....

Tabitha felt the sheets being pulled back opening her eyes. She saw Pete looking over her naked body and placed his mouth at one stage where he shouldn't but she was too out of it to even speak. He tried to help her to the bathroom but she fell on the floor in a heap, Pete was holding her in a way he was actually feeling her body rather than helping her but he was out if himself and Tabitha had history with him years ago on going home to his mums house with him one evening. He had sworn her to secrecy, but that wasn't the problem as she forgot him but somehow knew she knew him from before but could not place the memory. At that moment Johnny came in and said what's going on man what ru doing ? Upon then having to call Ryan to come help left her to the bed once again. On placing her on the bed once more a small towel was thrown to cover her body. She was again left to sleep it off while the others sat round the pool in the garden enjoying the night. Or patio perhaps, she could hear not see where they were from laying on the bed.

Roughly a hr later she was awoken again this time she felt the sheet being pulled slowly down she could feel herself naked with heavy eyes she opened them and Ryan was stood over her taking photos with his large camera. It had a big flash reflector. She had a silly sense of humor so she allowed him to take his erotic photos, but never if she had been sober, he lowered the camera close to her body so she allowed him to take some close ups of whatever he wished.

She sat up feeling dizzy and said let me see your camera, he jokingly cuddled it to say no im quite attached to it, he held it on his lap as he sat on the bed next to her. She noticed he was being coy, she asked him "are you hard"? He replied I might be.. Holding his camera tighter. She reached over to take hold of the camera to look at this her hand brushing with the back of her hand she could feel she was right.. Ryan told her Johnny had gone off with another woman to bed, so she thought well if that's the case she won't be waiting for him any longer to come to bed to sleep. She knew at this point she wouldn't bother trying to see him again. So between the flirting and the fact Ryan was aroused from taking the photos, she moved herself across the bed laying face down naked her chin resting on her hands elbows on the bed. He said "don't lie like that " it was arousing him, so she flipped herself back on the pillows looking up at him. He said I better go get some sleep, Tabitha asked "will you hold my hand until I fall asleep?" So he sat back down and she did fall asleep for a moment, she woke up because he said "well now you're asleep," she jumped up again, tried to keep her eyes open, held his hand tightly she didn't want him to leave her alone. So they teased each other a little more, she asked again are you hard? It was in this moment he made his first move, pulled back the sheets, placed his finger inside her asking are you wet? Then he sucked his finger.. To her pleasant surprise " Did you just taste me?" he replied"

Yes, it was weird sorry.. !" -Tabitha; "no not at all I havent lived nobody has ever done that before, can you taste me again"… this time he takes his mouth down and gives her one deep lick inside her all the way up the clitorus. Thats it shes wide awake, WOW! She says now youve made me horney I want to be fucked, just fucked ! Ryan said " not in his bed, get on the floor,"- so she lays down on the floor, he twirls her over telling her where to place her legs so he can take her how he wants it. Before she's even ready he's deep up inside her. It takes her breath away, he reaches down cuping and caressing her breasts, this shock wave of pleasure flows through her entire body like she's never felt before, probably he was the best she's ever had in her entire life. In Fact a definite yes to this being a fact. She collapses forward and can't keep upright as he's so thrustful, she flips over and says lets do it this way I'm too drunk. He didn't want that missionary position; he wanted her on top, as if she was capable of that but she'll give it ago. He lays down on the floor she straddles him slowly sliding down onto him, with every bit her body tingling she couldn't contain what she was feeling physically. She couldn't stay upright was too much to drink to keep up with him, he ended up taking control holding her up in the air with his strong arms and thrusting from below, she's never had it done this before, not only was he showing her things she had never tried or experienced he was blowing her mind away with every push inside her..He wasn't small either, He slowed down "I'm going to come!!!!" she wasn't capable of helping him she was in a heap from pleasure she couldnt move, she replied so am I infact I've been orgasaming the entire time ... the pleasure seemed endless even with a peak it kept going for her. Something she only experienced that one and only time.

As she lay on top of him just about to kiss she passed out. She was abruptly woken by Pete running in catching them he was mad he grabbed her threw her outside and argued with Ryan.

He then came out to comfort her, tears in his eyes, Tabitha what are you doing?- but she was all over the place and couldn't stand up by this point ready to pass out again. Pete went from angry to affection of holding her close to tears in his eyes saying how he liked her, he was then all over her too she wasn't really sure what was happening at this stage her head was spinning intensely.

Then The door opens and out comes Johnny at this point, he's fuming mad, he pulls Pete off her and punches him 3 times, then angrily pushes Tabitha onto the ground in temper. Hes crying holding his hands up" I really fucking liked you, you bitch,....... Fuck You."!!!

By this time she's crying and they're fighting. Pete goes back inside after saying his sorrys to Johnny, and Johnny picks her up from the gravel drive and walks her back to bed.

Some time goes by and petes at it again. She wakes up and he's inside her, she doesn't know if he's finished or just that moment for him, he then gets up and walks off. She goes back to sleep there isn't any way she can think properly or understand whats happening to her, there is a possibility she had been spiked back in the bar earlier, but ended up going home with Johnny was a bit of luck it took her out of harm's way from whoever had slipped something in to her drink.

Some time in the early hours Tabitha woke stubbled to the door she could hardly focus her eyes but she found a nightgown swung it on and wondered into the living room found Jonny sitting with his friends she sat across his lap and her legs swung over the arm, she played with his hair a while while Ryan had a fit of laughter after she said something she was too drunk to even know what she was saying. Ryan was taking photos again of the pair then he escorted her back to the bed he slowly removed the gown, he said " i'm not looking, "she knew he was looking by the way he took the gown off her so gently. She was standing there naked while Jonny and Ryan both tucked her in and off she went to sleep. She didn't stay asleep for long, she was up wrapped herself in the white sheet again and wondered into this time finding Jonny asleep in his armchair next to the fireplace, and Pete wide awake sitting on a wooden stool holding a tumbler glass, Pete looked angry go back to bed, he knew if she waked Jonny all hell would break loose. She kneeled down and woke him gently and asked him to come back to bed but he was too upset by her antics earlier. She couldn't recall what she did. So she got up to leave the room, after walking through the doorway to the hall she suddenly realised she was naked somehow she had lost the sheet along the way. Kath was standing at the end of the hall chatting with Ryan. Tabitha said help where is the bedroom as she covered herself with her hands as much as she could, kath pointed to the bedroom door, she was so intoxicated she couldn't see her way around the house. She looks up see's Ryan says it's a man turn around he turns and runs into a wall, she laughs as he then spins and runs into the kitchen to give her privacy. She then hears a" A'hem " its pete peering round the corner of the doorway holding the sheet he's still sitting in the chair, as she left the room he stamped on the sheet finding it hilarious she lost it, Johnny's standing up legs wide spread hands on his hips and they all burst out laughing as she turns pivot and runs naked into the bedroom and jumps under the covers. Right behind her standing in the bedroom doorway is Jonny, he says firmly "NOW STAY THERE AND GO TO SLEEP!"

CHAPTER FIVE

The morning arrives she's woken by Kath standing over her holding a coffee, which she places next to the bed but Tabitha falls back asleep.. The coffee was cold by the time she could bring herself to open her eyes. She felt someone jump on the bed. It was Jonny "hi," smiles laying next to her still in his clothes from the night before. She closes her eyes again, hears him muttering `` ok no, you're not awake and off he goes out the room.

She finally awakes sitting up. There was a pile of clothes at the end of the bed placed neatly folded for her. A bra, tracky bottoms, a t shirt, trainers and socks.. All she needs for the worst hangover ever. She wanders into the en suite to use the bathroom not to freshen up as she intends to get out of there fast she has no idea where she is; Johnny comes back in and waves his arms as if to say ok i'll come back in a minute.. She pulls on the clothes and wanders through the hall past the living room past the dining room. She turns a corner and sees a glass door looking out to a big garden, nearly mowed white picket fence and a pool. She walks into the kitchen where kath is sitting drinking her coffee ready suited and booted for work. Tabitha said"you look great and I look like i've been dragged through a hedge backwards, -"is this your house ?" No, her reply its johnny's do you like him- he likes you?"which ones Johnny Tabitha replies the one with long hair and she holds her own hair to describe him,, kath nods. At this she said yes I like him as a friend he's funny.

. "AS A FRIEND"? Johnny shouts from behind her startling her. She turns and says hey where did u go last night I was looking for you and goes to grab his shoulders as she did when he was sitting on the bench the night before. They talked for a while about a elephant painting on his kitchen wall to which Tabitha just folded her amrs to look up at saying it felt child like, a big fuck you from Johny for insulting it which she wasnt just a artist view of it.

She felt like she needed to get out of there, Jonny went off to go get washed and changed, Tabitha tried to take a swift exit her chance to go so she went out the wrong door and couldn't figure out how to leave this place. She walked around the pool, at this point Ryan came outside and said good morning last night was interesting smiling.. She had no memory of the night before she explained this to him briefly so awkwardly she said I need to get out of here. He opened the door to let her inside and to lead her to the front door; it was hidden behind a large heavy curtain. No wonder she couldn't find her way out; she thought it was a window. Ryan opened the door holding back the curtain for her to pass by, as she did so he leaned in to give her that kiss he was meant to give her the night before. This surprised her, she looked up at him shyly asking if something happened last night between us but he didnt say he just looked at her and raised one eyebrow. As she was leaving he followed her outside and said come again won't you be smiling. She looked back, smiled and walked away. She ended up wandering the wrong way again on the land completely disoriented, still she wandered up to Johnny's dad's place, complimenting how lovely is front decking was reminded her of a John Wayne's house from the old movie, he had seen her and his son the night before her sitting with her legs over his on the bench saying about time you two got together. So John, Johnny's father said good morning Tabitha. I'd offer you a coffee but I have none. Did you sleep well? I think so, yes but I don't know where Johnny vanished. She said her goodbyes and found her way to the end of the drive and started to make the long walk home, hitch hiking being the only way. She's not got far when a small old car approaches her.. It's Johnny .. but even by this point she already had forgotten who he was. He shouted to get in the car. "Why didn't you wait for me? " - I didn't even have time to dry my hair while holding his wet locks in his hand.

She was perplexed; she had already forgotten him from ten mins ago.. Her mind wiped clean already. He joked in the car on the way taking her back to her car in the next town. He said be ready for the news you be all over it naked walking down the road as he laughed .. She thought he was joking. But he was right, there were the photos of her naked holding Johnny's hand walking the road in the middle of the night totally out of it all over facebook.

His Commitment…..

Two months had passed and she received a knock at the door there standing a giant bouquet of flowers, the biggest she had ever seen,it brought her to her knees in fact as she had no boyfriend for the last six months or so and wondered who it might be..

Standing in the garden was a stranger (it was Johnny) but to her she was already a stranger she had no memory of him. His hair was orange and curtly long,she reached out to touch it asking why is it this colour it was clearly dried nobody had that natural. He replied " don't look at the hair ignore it, it's going back". He said the flowers are from me, he leaned in to kiss her and she blacked away. Are you trying to kiss me? He said yes, she replied but I don't know you,, he looked confused. She was even more confused and said you have bad timing. I've just found out I'm pregnant but he already knew this by his reaction. I think the head, heart and the flowers were just because of the baby. Ryan was sitting in the car parked outside looking in. Johnny went back to the car and jumped in the back seat.

They stayed parked there for a hr or so watching and chatting to her in her garden she was saying why are you here to them? There was another man with them but she can't recall him yet. Ryan jumped out the car and held the seat forward signalling for her to go sit in and talk to Johnny. She sat facing the back, facing johnny. He undid her jeans slightly and placed his hands on her pregnant belly he was teared up. He Just sat there saying nothing at first then he spoke;" I have to go away for a few months but I'd like to come back and check on you and the baby if that's ok?". Why she replied, why would you do that, it's not your baby (she didn't remember sleeping with him or Ryan.)Ryan is looking down at her. They spent some time that afternoon chatting. Johnny kept shouting to not lift anything, don't lean over the fence, you'll hurt the baby. He seemed overly worried about her baby. As she got up from the car Ryan reached out and placed his hand on her belly saying take care of that baby with concern for it !!! smiling at her as she walked away.

She had no idea what had gotten into these two men or why they were being so protective. She sat in her front garden and she could see they were taking photos of her, she was sitting with her children enjoying the sun as they drove away.

CHAPTER SIX

During the next month her family found out she was pregnant and her ex who was now seeing her aunt ganged with her to force Tabitha into a abortion. It wasnt his baby to bully her into a abortion. Her aunt said, ''Are you going to get rid of that baby or do you want me to punch it from your stomach on several occasions? She offered Taabitha a drink to make the baby in her words slip away. After this didn't work she beat her up stamping her high heels into her belly with another woman joining in together she believes they killed the baby, the next day she woke up in agony bleeding. The police arrived to take photos of her stomach as there was a clear heel mark on her stomach from the attack. They kept threatening you cant consider keeping this baby, he told me he hates that you're pregant says you a stupid fucking bitch. She visited Tabitha daily passing on these malicious false awful messages for her to get rid of the baby, even the ex joined in with her bullying her to get rid of it as Johnny didn't want her pregnant. They slowly wore her down telling her he's decided to take the baby if she keeps it for her. She caved and reluctantly beliving these two story she booked a abortion. The morning she arrived at the hospital Jonny was there screaming and shouting abuse, sadly she didn't recognise him again no memory or who he was she just knew her aunt had told her she would beat the baby out of her if she didn't go ahead with it.

Jonny's screaming so much she can't even focus in the hospital waiting area. While in the bed waiting she had a change of heart. She wanted to change her mind but the drs were rushing her, inside she decided to keep the baby and went to get dressed to leave to be told hun you've already been in for the procedure ... she couldn't even comprehend why the memory loss had happened again so fast . on leaving the hospital jonny was waiting outside he shouted you fukcing bitch you fucking murderer ... to which she looks back at him and collapses. Sitting on the curb.

When she arrives home shes distraught with grief being forced into abortion at 12 weeks she could feel the baby doing suppersalts already kicking frantically and held her pain stricken womb she was crying for a good 10 days over this to the point the dr had to given her valium. The loss of a child she wanted to keep was too much. It was bullied from her own choice taken away by others selfishness to not allow her to be happy. She didn't waste time to start seeing someone else and soon fell pregnant again soon after in grief she was taken advantage of her vulnerable ness by a man she detested and who physically made her feel sick.

Months went by, Tabitha was in Tesco shopping with her toddler, Jonny walked by and looked at her in shock shouts "you bitch you killed mine to go put another one in there"! he was raging lashing out kicking towards her and her child. She was infuriated and shouted at him to back off in a rage to protect herself. She was wearing a pair of maternity dungarees feeling heavy from the baby growing so big. He quickly waved both arms back away and said sorry looking very upset. Tabitha thought he was just a case of mistaken identity; she had no idea who he was. - Still

Of all the hundreds of hours and nights spent with this man since she was a young girl she couldn't hold onto anything, she just thought she was skatty and forgetful but nobody sat her down and explained it. Her family knew but decided to keep it a big secret from her, never helping her just interfering. It wasn't long before Tabitha decided they were not healthy to be around and walked away from her family, preferring to be alone to live her life and she was much happier once she made that move.

During the pregnancy she was around a few months in, one afternoon jonny appeared in her doorway, "hi" i've brought you a gift, "a gift?" she was confused thinking he must be a delivery man but she accepted. He went out to his car and carried in a painting with delicate paper wrapped over it, I hope you like it, there's something on the back to help jog your memory, Well I hope it does. It's ok if you don't know yet it may come later please keep it safe. She turns it around reading on the back in large spiky handwriting all the places they had slept together one of the nights she went to his place but couldn't recall. On the back It read;- Against a Wall, In the Grass, In a Trunk, and alone in my Bed. He stepped back a little nervous looking his hands holding up to his mouth like in a praying position, he waited intently the moment for her to remember something, but she turned to look at him and thanking him blankly, I love it thank you but she had no idea what it meant or who he was, she still did not recall this man at all. Not even all the years and time they spent together he was wiped away like he never existed.

Roughly a few weeks on, something similar happened again, she was at home, a knock at the door, there stood Ryan this time standing on her step facing out he turned to look at her as the door opened, he looked mad, "you're pregnant", it seemed he was angry, this stranger frightened her she was sure if he was going to hurt she was used to having strangers sent round to do random attacks, so was nervous this might be another one of those. He realised by the look on her face he had startled her, he had no idea she didn't know him or remember him he was talking presuming she knew who he was. She was just standing there trying to understand what on earthy this stranger was mad at her for being pregnant or why ?" We need to talk" he spouted, "do you want to come in,?" he seemed upset there was a man standing with a camera the press it seemed but she didnt understand why the press were following him. He stood in the doorway and placed his hand on her pregnant belly, turned and smiled lets give him a photo he called her close to his side, Tabitha laughed thought how silly but ok she was calmed and released he wasn't there to be mad at her but she wanted to find out why he was there. He came into her kitchen, he took a seat, she stood holding her bump with her hands as he seemed agitated again, "are you going to hurt me"? She asked, he looked up from the floor, NO, course not, looking at her bump. He looking around said, "you can't stay here or raise the child here you'll have to come to canada, I'll get you a house you need a big house i'll provide for all of you I guess, but there will be rules I need to see this child and have equal part in its upbringing. "I'm not moving to Canada, I don't know anyone there !" - "this child will need protection and this is what's best for it. At that Tabitha said something that upset him, he slammed down two DVD's on to her kitchen side demanded she watch them and she'll understand, they were films with him in, but it wasn't that she didn't remember, he didn't realise it was complete memory losses due to several reasons beyond her control, she wasn't doing this on purpose he didn't exist in her memory as a man, he didn't exist even though she'd met him several times she simply wasn't holding onto new memories as well, it affected her organising it affected her not turning up to events she had forgot she agreed to go to over the years, she just presumed she was scatty but it went deeper, being left this way and her family were informed years earlier about her amnesia but they decided to keep it a big secret from her instead of helping they added to the confusion, gaslighting her to cause more harm than good for their own selfish reasons or gains. This was unforgivable. So at that Ryan stormed out very upset slamming the door behind himself on the way out. He left a note inside one of the DVD's for her, but before she ever got to read it they had gone missing. Some things just don't have answers, and fate kept putting blocks in her way of progress.

When she had her youngest baby in the hospital Jonny and his mum and his gf came to the hospital to support her, Ryan also had flown all the way from Canada he explained d requesting to do a dna test. Tabitha had the abortion but they didnt belive her as she'd fallen preg so soon after. So curious to see if either of them was the father. They both held her. The baby girl had black hair and blue eyes, she could hear Jonny screaming in the corridor she's not mine man, blue eyes and too big. He cried out "its like losing it all over again as he sobbed. "He came held Tabithas hand as he did so she passed out from the drugs of the c section. -So they thought but something more serious was amiss.

She woke for short bursts during the hospital stay Jonny had organised a private room. The press were sitting in the corridor. Jonny's mother was waiting. She popped her head in and asked can she hold the baby, yes she replied of course and her eyes were heavy and couldn't stay awake. was being looked after for three days by Jonny, he was there feeding her while Tabitha slept for three days solid. She want allowed to breast feed which was confusing. She couldn't keep her eyes open. She was seriously unwell. Jonnys mum said how will she take care of the baby if she sleeps all day, unbeknown them she wasn't sleeping she was drugged up the nines by a mentally ill woman who had come to the hospital claiming to be a social worker posing illegally and spiking Tabitha's water jug.-she kept asking the nurse why is her water dirty it looks like sand in the bottom. The nurse said I'll take it away and get it tested, she looked concerned and suspicious because she was complaining about the dirty water jug for 3 days.

On the nurses hasty return she looked alarmed, she took the baby to the nursery then took Tabitha out in the hall, placed a clean jug of water in the room and looking back carefully the nurse caught the ill woman dropping a handful of some powder into Tabitha's water jug . She confronted the woman but she struggled with her then she threw the jug across the room.. The nurse asked her to leave.

Tabitha was taken back to her bed, she was woken by the mentlly ill women pulling back her bed sheets nad punching her in her c section, at this point a police woman arrived and told the women to leave on her being dragged out the room the twisted women kicked the new born baby's crib with her in it across the room with a heavy jolt almost tipping it in a attempt the kill the baby. Tabitha jumped up, pulled the cord and asked for help, she felt dizzy and coulndt stay awake . After a period of time the mentally ill woman forced her way back to Tabitha's side she grabbed the baby and forced a dirty bottle of water into the baby's mouth which was laced with drugs that had been keeping Tabitha asleep for 3 days. Upon rang the bell for help. The nurse rushed the baby to special care after being told what this woman had done to it,.. She later came to Tabitha saying with a deep look of worry on her frown, we can't wake the baby. We are very sorry we will do our best with your permission but it's not not looking good prepare yourself . Tabitha told her to go do what she had to do to wake the baby. Later that evening she was awake and all was fine, but the nurses suspected the mentally ill woman had drugged her as well as in a twisted mental episode.

During the stay just before Jonny left to say his goodbyes from the hospital visit helping her out, feeding the baby, Jonny grabbed Tabitha by her hand walking her into the bathroom where he ran her a bath requesting she lay down and laid some towels for her on the floor . He watched her bathe,during standing over her gazing down he became aroused and offered "do you want another one in there- I can help with that if you like?" Tabitha turned to him " what ru saying exactly ru offering me a baby to stay pregnant he replied yes?"… he laid down a towel and pillow and pointed in a wave to the floor undoing his belt on his jeans and smiled. So before they knew it these two are like magnets whenever they meet they end up in bed together or perhaps should say every place on earth including a bed. She lays down and he lays on top of her, you'll have to do all the work, she requests due to her c-section, she wasn't capable of using her tummy muscles yet,.... well so he did, on his withdrawal she could tell immediately she was pregnant again.

Deja vu……..

Three months pass, Jonny turns up at her house again standing in the same spot he had before hand on her tummy he looks side to side then says "deja vu, you are pregnant !" T-"no I cant be, I haven't had sex yet, "? in dismay rolls her eyes and has a deep think how can I be I feel my tummy is hard although I dont rem having sex ".. he then shouted "you drugged me "! She laughs at such a ludicrous idea as if she wouldn't have a clue how to do that, let alone waste money while she's trying to give birth. Nothing made sense because she couldn't recall the hospital time or him even visiting her. The memory is gone again just like that poof ! In fact what had happened was Johnny was drinking from Teresa's water jug in the hospital unbeknown to them both the mentally ill woman had spiked it in her deluded jealous rage of poisonous minded sickness she was suffering from. According to her medical treatment the woman had psychosis . more like something more serious perhaps undiagnosed to how sick she really was attempting to kill a new baby twice. A Couple weeks later Tabitha lost the baby while breast feeding her youngest child. She felt a sharp pain pressure and the tiny baby came away all intact in its sack umbilical cord and placenta all attached so perfectly formed but it just didn't make it. The health visitor came and discussed this, asking her who her boyfriend was at the hospital and the nurses had heard them in the bathroom so a rumour had already got around who the father was. Still unbeknown to her she had no idea what the nurse was chatting about and dismissed it as a mistake.

CHAPTER SEVEN

The flashbacks now she was experiencing she couldn't understand why she had them about Johnny, it didn't make sense as she thought flashbacks were about painful things but Jonny had never hurt her, in fact they never really got emotionally close they just had fun together. She recalled he gave her her first tattoo, on her shoulder a shamrock when she was young before she had kids, probably 18. She used to bump into him and hang with him a lot. They knew each other really well over the years.

Silly little memories here there and everywhere things you'd expect, they'd meet on the bus to go to the town, they'd go driving around places have funny banter always joking about hardly ever serious with each other just laughed a lot at their random meetings it began to feel like the world was very small indeed.

Tabitha would turn up to her baby scans and there was Johnny in the background at every single one he was even accusing her first born and several other pregnancies of being his, to actually paying for a copy of one for himself to keep, which to her was very confusing he was still a stranger to her, why would a stranger want her scan photos and Once he saw her heavily pregnant their meetings were a little too close. He would be there in the background looking over and often ask her how the baby is doing. "Is everything ok?"he asked, she would look at him and wonder why this strange man is asking about my baby. It was like he seemed to know she had memory loss, if he didnt he must have been as confused as she was.

Let's go back again.....

So life went on Tabitha got to her late 20s, she decided to join another lady to stringfellows for an evening out not sure exactly the day but it was a week night as it wasn't very busy. They arrived and bought a couple drinks. Tabitha went to sit down, walking down the steps to the red seats tilted looking down at the stage, facing the large speakers by the dance floor. She sat alone, the other lady had gone to chat to Sid Ower was his name, they were having a blast up stairs so Tabitha left her to it. She heard a voice saying hello nice to meet you and an outstretched arm welcomed her to his club. It was stringfellow wearing a white blazer and his white hair in a ponytail. He said this is my club. I always like to welcome a beautiful woman to my club. Hello I'm Peter and you are > ? "Tabitha,...." she replied, smiling back and swiftly shaking his hand. He walked down to the speakers and placed his ear to it but walked away holding his ears in his hands shaking his head.

A Few mins later Tabitha's friend comes down the steps, shouts come up here, but it's very loud she couldn't hear her well but recognised when she was being beckoned . Do a curtsy now to him introducing her to a tall blond man who says he's A Prince, curtsy, Tabitha said no I'm not bowing to nobody thinking its a joke. He smiles and begins to chat.. But she walks back down the steps and sits alone again after a quick hello to the man. He follows her down the steps then approaching her asks her to come talk to him he's standing very tall on the above step looking down at her, she looks up ad says you're nice, definitely my type, blond hair, blue eyes, and gives him a smile, then turns to go sit again, and he mentions .. -"That's inappropriate, come back here I haven't given you permission to walk away ."!. She could tell he was joking around due to his smirking so she walks back close to him really looking closely over his features and he's quite handsome. He asks her how old do you think I am?................, Tabitha>? Hmm..29? Going by your hair line I'd say 29 yes.." I'm 21.!" ….…..Oh sorry,... she always puts her foot in it . Prince Louis;" it's genetics.….. unfortunately."

His Royal Highness Prince Louis was now playing little pranks on Tabitha, "I'm in a slight predicament. I'm being chased by these two unsavoury men. I need to get out fast, safely to my home. Have you got a car, could you possibly help? " yes my cars outside," in that moment the two men came running past, so in a attempt to hide he said quick hide me throwing his arms round her cuddling into her neck with his face, but she feels he is gently kissing her neck he pulls back then grabs her pulling her round the waist tightly kisses her passionately, embracing her his hands are up and down her back slowly feeling her slight curves, she's quite slim, in great shape she used to regularly visit the gym to keep herself tightly in shape. He then stands back, still holding her hands gazing deeply into her eyes, "Your eyes are stunning", he leans in for another kiss,… she pulls back for a moment looks up at him smiling," well I've heard it all now that's the funniest chat up line I've ever had and he shrugs his shoulders then kiss one more time. Suddenly in the moment he removes his sweater," i'm getting a little hot and wraps it over her shoulders. He says quick lets go, reaching out and grabs her by the hand as they run to her car just outside the club. The two men were chasing them, calling him shouting ``come back Prince Louis"!. We just want to talk. They ran outside, it's lightly raining, the weather was warm but the drizzle made the evening chilly. She jumps in the car, he's frantically trying the car handle. Why isn't it opening? She laughs " it doesn't have central locking, " still smiling at how the other half live. This amused her how he was so used to the luxurys of a new car. In that moment of thought she reaches over and unlocks the door. The Prince requests" quickly the men are there dont look up Tabitha don't look up" but she did. One of them is holding a black curvy bladed knife so she locks the door quickly. Tabitha turns to the man holding the knife "you coward ! pulling a knife, youre pathetic, now Fuck off ! " aggressively she shouts, by this time the other man grabbed him round the neck and pulled him back giving her a wink to get away. It feels like a wind up as he could have opened the door at any opportunity so she had an inkling it was fake.

"Tabitha you should definitely join the army you don't seem to have fear." No she laughs I can't take orders. " He shouts "drive quickly go go, "she drops the keys then recovers herself starts the engine, slams it in gear and spins around in a circle facing the opposite direction within seconds, Tabiath was a confident driver she knew how to handle bikes and cars at speed, from her earlier days of doing handbrake turns and donuts just for fun she often raced too, had a few wins under her belt so he picked the right person to drive him although intoxicated, this didn't hinder her reflexes. He points the directions. -" It's about a mile "… well i'm going to get lost now i'll never find my way home oh well, she laughs .. . They drive past all the London black cabs in a long row each side of the road as they drive down the middle she had never seen this before, it was eye opening to see so many as she was a untravelled girl from the countryside, look at all them i've never seen that many cabs all at once, he briefly explained who uses them,, they drive around this monument and see Buckingham Palace.. He has her driving through parts she's concerned she isn't allowed to go but he insists it's the right way. She begins to spin the car around in circles in the large open space outside the Palace just a couple of laps of honour she laughs, he shouts" STOP!" are you kidnapping me, stop! she laughs "no I am not kidnapping you silly, finding him hilarious I'm just looking at it all from all angles I wont see it again." They pull up outside Buckingham Palace, she parks the car, switches off the engine, they sit and talk for a while. He takes off his sweater again and throws in the back seat offering it as a souvenir. "So Louis, that's your name right?" -yes! they small talk for a short period but she's a champion at subject change. He leans towards her " you're hot!" In that moment he leans in for another prolonged kiss to which they both enjoy, the heat between them was intense. This went on for sometime, some heavy petting the heat of the moment. Passion definitely wasn't the place in this small car with no space but the tension being imminent, he was aware there were cameras all round and the two men following behind parked up 50 feet away. Watching . Louis spoke up" don't worry those are my friends'', it's ok we were just messing around it's something I do for entertainment, sorry about that but she saw the funny side of it. Back in the club Peter Stringfellow had snapped loads of photos of her with Prince Louis kissing her, also some random ones with himself, Tabitha standing behind him with a few other women, she stood on the end back right looking like a deer in the headlights she thought after it appeared on the internet one day. For a dull week night it was certainly entertaining. Peter said Tabitha '' let me shake your hand again", and don't you forget he chose you. I'm a witness to that and I want to be the first person to take your photo as he smiled widely with a cheeky grin on his face. In Fact he was actually quite a sweet kind man.

So the kissing with wandering hands on both they were both locked into the moment all their surroundings seemed to fall back away they were totally in it the world outside disappeared while their lips were gliding over each other, it started to become a little intense. Louis took a breath as their hands were pushing all the right buttons on each other. They wanted to go further but he was concerned for cameras and being caught, " I want to show you my bedroom,"he perked, "Really"? -I can't go in there, yes you can if you're with you will be fine. "What will you do if I show you my bedroom i mean to me what will you do ?" Tabitha; " can't lie will probably rip your clothes off and be all over you"- then what he asks ?.. Then you'll take off all my clothes and we'll see what happens from there .. as she laughs but means every word and he knew it, and he wanted it as much as she did… he jumped forward with that," come on let's go, but be extremely quiet do not make a sound.. So they leave the car and he leads her down the narrow path with a perfectly trimmed hedge row along her right hand side, he leads her on through the kitchen door to the left. This kitchen is huge and she can't believe her eyes. There were so many pots and pans hanging from an arch ceiling, " how many pans do you really need,"? The absolute rubbish couldn't believe what was coming from her mouth, she thought to herself, just shut up now before you ruin it woman. -"yes They are all needed," concentrate, but she was all over the shot… he takes her through a doorway into a hallway (clearly it's not called a hallway) lots of stairs, red carpet she suddenly stops in fear, i can't go through here.]

He grabs her by the shoulders Tabitha "- I am Prince Louis The Duke of Cambridge"! You can come in here as you're with me. It will be fine. then embraces and kisses her again as she was standing there in shock. Something that snapped her out of a jaw dropping trance.

"Now look at those stairs over there, we need to make a run for the red staircase behind me ok?" She looks over can hardly focus there was so much for her eyes to take in she couldn't process it all at once, " I cant run in stilettos up those stairs", he grabs her shoulders and turns her not those stairs, those ones with the corner they go round the corner twisting her to a different view point. -"Oh ok" .. then shes destreacted by the large painting, how on earth did you get that in the door it's as big as a entire wall .. he grabs her again says its in a scroll flat pack oh makes sense she replies she's wondering why is she talking about the painting ~at a moment like this?

At that moment they hear a noise: it's Her Majesty The Queen. Is that you Louis she calls out in her nightgown holding a walking stick she emerges from the lift behind the stairs. She thinks it was a lift she couldn't see round the corner as she didnt see her coming down any of the staircases. He replied "yes grandmother please go back to bed sorry to disturb you. " Tabitha says I'm so sorry for waking you. Louis grabs her again '' don't talk to her like that," like what ?-oh sorry, and suddenly realises she was supposed to be courteous and was just being her normal self and totally forgot her manners.

This time they attempt to run up the stairs but he hears footsteps hastily in fear of being caught they turn and run back down, quick we must hide. He leads her down the stairs and running fast in his nightgown and slippers is His Majesty Prince Arthur, running towards us pointing fiercely red faced and very angry shouting "GET OUT< GET OUT! "!.. they run back through the kitchen into a dark room.. Louis is kissing her again against the wall, she giggles and gives away their hiding place.

The door opens its Prince Arthur, again or should I say still angry shouting to get out. Tabitha turns to him in disbelief; she wants to take a deep long look at him but he's too mad to let her have that moment to take it all in. -"sorry I'm leaving. " Louis turns to his father; '' Father calm down, remember your blood pressure." then he grabs Tabitha by the hand walking her out the kitchen door to the path outside he apologises "I'm very sorry about that", it's fine she replies,

I totally understand I was never allowed men to come into my house either, I'm used to strict parents, Louis said this is slightly different in comparison but that's not a bad thing having a strict upbringing. She agreed she was lucky. Prince Arthur was standing there buttoned up to the very top, they were like perfectly ironed, a crested nightgown, crested slippers all very neat, he wore smarter clothes to bed than most men wear on a night out. A Shame he was so angry, but it's not like he's ever going to sit and put the kettle on for her.

So Louis walked Tabitha back to the car, " scoot over ", as she climbed in through the passenger side, climbed over the handbrake into the driver's seat. He got in next to her which gave her comfort realising he really was the Perfect Gentleman. They sat chatting about His mother and his father, he was so heartfelt she could sense how dearly he loved her, how much he missed her. Tabitha talked about how she believed that Prince Arthur loved his wife, she remembers the news they looked so happy.. He gave his opinion on this too, he opened up so much he was such a lovely man for someone so young he seemed to know what he wanted in life an old wise head on a young man's shoulders. Tabitha wont go into too much detail of what went on the conversation was deep, the moment was "unforgettable" and oddly enough she never forgot him or that night of all things she managed to hold onto she's glad it was him. She claims she's the luckiest woman in England to have had that night happen to her. He told her to never tell or they would both be in catastrophic trouble. They sat and talked, kissing until the sun came up the next morning.. ~ Perhaps a little more than kissing went on that night, but she shall never tell,as she smiles thinking back to that wonderful night.~ She will never be able to top this one!

Just as he was about to step out of the car and say goodbye this brought a feeling of sadness, She called to him can I have one last kiss if i'm never going to see you again?"

It happened so fast. Don't drive away until I'm safely in the door. I'm a little afraid he smirked, another example of his sense of humour. As he waved her off she drove back past the black cabs ass she did so the police coming in the opposite direction waved her to stop, on doing so she wound down the window. One of the policemen shouted, "Do you have a stow away in the form of a Prince in your boot ?......."We hope you haven't kidnapped him laughed, then waved her off.

The long hangover drive home was a joy thinking about it took away all the suffering as Tabitha smiled all the way home. Thinking how lucky she was. She went home to bed, snuggling his sweater until she fell asleep. She would often wear it to bed to keep warm then remember her moment even if it was short lived it all had to be kept a secret at least for many years she kept silent anyway. It began to eat away to not mention so this is why it's here now. This was roughly two weeks before Louis's birthday, Tabitha's car appeared on the news titled; who was the mystery woman dropping off prince Louis early hrs of the morning. The only way to get a photo of the car from behind was the two body guards who followed them.

CHAPTER EIGHT

Let's go back to the school days, of what Tabitha was good at, Art and Daydreaming she laughs telling her story. Well,- I was fairly fit I guess, but then who isn't at 15, you're at your peak strong and able in those days, the world is your oyster. I was young and free with no commitments just how I Liked it she adds

- She had one friend called Ella Mae, this was her best friend right from the age of five. They are still close today even though their lives are busy they stay in touch. There would be days they would have been about 11 or 12 they both lived in a rural village 3 miles apart. Now next door to Ella Mae lived Georgo Martin, he was the manager of a famous band in the 60s, he was a kind man, Ella Mae and Tabitha would often ride their bikes and meet half way down the country lane. Then sit and chat for a couple of hours, bringing the world to rights, or talking about school, or who they had crushes on; pop stars and the smash hits and just 17 Magazine. Then say goodbye, see you at school monday, before riding home again. Funny little part of their independence as they strayed away at the beginning venturing into the world as young growing women.

So back to George, he used to let the villagers use his pool. He would let them use his Rolls Royce for weddings if they married in the church next door. He was kind to Tabitha. He dwelled in a large stately home but he never looked down on people.

The two girls as older teenagers by now would often gate crash his parties in later life meeting no end of stars; Tony Hetter being one of them, a famous artist from a tv show. Tabitha always wanted to be one, but she wasn't quite good enough to go pro, but good enough for a hobby which was satisfying to her nevertheless. Tabitha had a funny moment with Paul Mckart he was one of the band members that george managed, she bumped into him as he came out from the bathroom in a pub, in a tiny little space they exchanged a lovely little chat he was very pleasant to talk to in fact he left an ~impression to last.

So Ella Mae along with Tabitha would have grown a little older to the point she had a motorbike, on having this great idea to try and rev it hard up a steep hill. The bike wasn't man enough so it flipped a wheelie and they fell off in a heap of laughter. Got back on with bent handlebars they carried on to the local pub they were off to that night. From the funny antics of growing up together swimming in the river Thames to walking miles to get places but the talks were the best. This was cut short when Ella Mae went off and got married very young. Tabitha wasn't the marrying kind, she couldn't settle no matter how hard she tried she was meant to be free. ~A rebel.

Going forth…

She was madly into her cars and motorbikes, she moved in as a lodger with a man called Robin Vin he became a friend for a short time, they spent some time at silverstone she was about 21 her first child was 6 months old. She went along in his vincent hurricane which was a remodel of the spitfire he and his brother designed a body kit from Fiberglass to fit perfectly on the old body to replace the rusting old body work but the shape was changed also.

They spent the day in the pits, Stirling Mosso was one side, Chris Re a pop star on the other side, but she didn't speak to him. Tabitha got to meet Stirling Mosso. He approached her, tapping her on the shoulder saying" I'm going to come chat with you after my race, smiling looking back as he walked away, then headed off to his car. Tabitha went for a good couple hours walking round the race track chatting to a friend of Robins. He was funny that's all she really remembers, oh, and he was small, built about the same size as Jonny actually. They had a fantastic day out. They came across the start of the race Stirling Mosso getting his car ready into position when Tabitha waved at him he waved his hand to hold on a moment as he got out to talk to her she asked for his signature after looking around asking for a pen so he could sign her leg. ~Her outfit, which is a skin tight all in one catsuit short in the legs for the weather was hot, she had borrowed some trainers to save her feet but they were too big but it didn't matter really.

The Stalker

Over the years Tabitha became aware she had a stalker, she couldn't quite figure out who it was for many years. Odd things would happen, threats left on her answerphone tapes. A woman saying she was going to kill Tabitha's kids, this tape was taken by the police and traced to a squat in oxford. It appeared it was a homeless junkie who'd become obsessed with her. It turned out she had a serious mental illness to which she kept getting away with her crimes, from prostiution, mugging people at cash machines, to shoplifting and attempting to stab a woman with a heroin needle to which took her off the streets for a couple years in prison but it didn't help her mentally. She came out even more messed up. Rea really had it in for the women she used to know in school it turned out Tabitha wasn't the only victim of her mental episodes. The woman had lost her own babies to care because she attacked the lady with the needle, so when she went to prison she couldn't look after it. By time she was out again she had another child they had to take that one due to it clicking as she was injecting heroin while pregnant. She blamed her boyfriend of course and was very convincing for a while to her friends but it soon became clear it was her who was the abuser in the relationship. The children had a lucky escape as rumour had it she was giving her first born heroin on the dummy to make it sleep. Pretty dark personally and a dangerous person to have as a friend or an enemy. Victims soon accumulated to give their experiences of her malicious antics.

Now this individual did things like stay up for days taking drugs writing satan all over her bedroom walls and ceiling, not a bit of clear wall was from the insane graffiti which rang big alarm bells early on age 16, her parents didn't get her help they kicked her out. So while they went on holiday she broke into their house and had all her homeless friends destroy the home, pulling wallpaper off stabbing sofas, microwaving the rabbit, ripped up the carpet, and smashed the tvs and robbed the house. On their return they had to call the police on her. That sums up the summary of her mental illness beginnings. Which went untreated for too long therefore never was dealt with properly at all.

She had some infatuation with Tabitha since around school leaving age. Rumour had it her father had abused her growing up by hitting around the head a lot, but not necessarily true, she was the type to falsely accuse men of things often so it became like cry wolf, nobody knows the truth but whatever happened or perhaps a chemical imbalance there is no excuse for how far her vindictiveness went to another level of beyond any forgiveness.

But when Rea lost her children her parents weren't allowed to adopt them but nobody knew why as they were extremely wealthy.

So over the years, Bea a little twisted rich girl had it all and still seemed to mess up her life. She had played one parent against the other during a bitter divorce and they both tried to outdo each other and bought her a house each. This wasn't enough for the wealthy family who were also claiming thousands in benefits, Bea had to accept her mental illness and lapped up the DLA bragging how she would exaggerate her mental depression to get top pay. She had never worked, only ever knew how to live off mummy and daddy. She would sit and gaze glazed eyes wide as she was wired all the time on whatever drugs she was prescribed it took her out of the room into another world of her own. But it didn't stop her plotting her attacks and the money she used to pay off homeless people or just anyone sick enough to get involved in her attacks on her victims. She would go as far as posing as a social worker to get into peoples houses on doing so she would steal from them during the room checks. Unknowing to the victims or notice cd's missing from the cases or jewellery anything a kleptomaniac could smuggle into her pockets. Perfume was her favourite steel.

Her home was cluttered with material items and riches but to a filthy state of disorder. Money left laying around all over the house too much money she didn't know what to do with it all. A spendaholic. So that's the long winded list of said symptoms. Now let's get down to the acts.

Committed sickness

Now Bea as we established had her moments over a 26 year period this went on for until she was discovered by her own mistake she accidently admitted spiking Tabitha due to the fact she accidentally spiked her own drink by mistake on this occasion, she reacted openly and aggressively by shouting" 1 spiked you" throwing a drink in Tabitha's face, but this was a day Tabitha was already in suspicion her malicious behaviour had developed to a unruly no limits point. She tried to avoid her as much as possible weaning her away only seen her once a year as she was becoming a nuisance wanting to know where Tabitha was going always calling her to a point she actually went as far as to fit a tracker in Tabitha's car which she accidently found looking for the diagnostics plug one day because the car was playing up. Tabitha had a plan and placed it into someone else's car to test bea. Low and behold she had a call asking her if she was at the airport but in fact it wasn't her. If that's not enough to give you the chills, the long list will it became her entire life doing something new each time. Bea would call and make fake calls to the landlord of Tabitha pretending to be her and one day her landlord turned up and evicted her for threatening them, bringing the police to evict, her with her six children onto the streets, she requested desperately " can you trace the call or email and find out whos doing this?"- but the landlord didn't believe she had a stalker which she'd written to on several occasions to help her. She felt she was being stalked but no help ever came.

So during the years, there was many red flags about Bea. She would call Tabitha to ask her what is she up to or where is she planning on going that day. To many a coincidence she would either Bea herself appear or her family members would be there just as Tabitha was arriving. Then the shouting and screaming would begin including assaults. Bea would stand back often glazed eyes watching with excitement the only time she could express any form of a feeling for a brief moment if something horrific was happening Bea would get off on it enjoying the chaos of trouble she had organised carefully planned she paid off individuals made up all kinds of stories to causes drama,the ~ manipulation queen.

Bea got braver and braver the more she got away with her bitterness the worse she became obsessed. She began to take photos of Tabitha and post flyers all round town the day she knew where Tabitha was going she was handing out flyers saying Tabitha didn't have custody of her own children and to try take them away if you see her, and her children were assaulted a few times, strangers had grabbed two of her toddlers on 2 occasions frightening them immensely then apologise deeply once the police had arrived. So soon after their arrival an apology was given although it was apparent it was not a prank. But nothing got done about it; the police let Tabitha down gravley.

Bea paid a man to beat and attack Tabitha's little boy in a play park, he pushed him off a high swing and kicked him on the ground the man was extremely drunk in the day time so it appears he was one of Beas drunk friends the circle she mixed in was mostly those of a feather in habits like herself a drug addict and alcoholic. Don't take that wrongly that it means just because they drink etc they're bad people of course there's equally good hearted souls who have addictions it was just this minority around Bea. Unfortunately>

There was a period where someone kept posting sausages through the letterbox of Tabitha's house during the early, ~Bea really was relentless. Did she never sleep?.. These were Planned for her dog to cause harm but one morning her toddler got hold of it and took a bite he became gravely ill. The drs said it was arsenic poisoning. Tabitha didn't know who was doing it so she installed a box to catch the post neither the dog or her son could get to. One day Bea came to visit, clearly Tabitha had no idea who it was at this point, this was when her first child was an only child. She caught Bea pulling off the box on Tabisha's door confronting her she acted oddly she would grunt she creeped Tabitha out, often she would avoid her or not answer the door in an attempt to wean her away. But just presumed it was her drug habit that made her act oddly. Tabitha didn't realise the real intention was to allow the poisonous substances into the house again to carry on with her obsessive sick plan to hurt the little boy.

Over a solid 11 year period Tabitha had a new car each year not brand new but new to her, within a matter of days it was damaged keyed up or kicked in..relentlessly she would call the police but to no avail or help given even tho it was clear someone had a mental obsession. She had a stalker but the Police kept letting her down each time she tried to get help. Tabitha would go to towns and catch Bea handing out flyers, on several occasions T was told Bea was seen buying drugs and warned by others that they feared Bea was dangerously planning something with bad intentions towards her. T brushed it off many times dismissing the facts and clues in front of her eyes handed to her on a plate were all the clues right there. On several different occasions~ Four men approached her telling her someone had tried to hire them to harm her, only she didn't believe it, blinded to it, trusted too much and never understood why someone would be wanting to hurt her children or target them. It just seemed so heinous and unbelievable. Which was a mistake she should have reported on long before things took a serious turn where it became too late to fix it. ~if only the CID were as good as FBI she thought? They would of had this solved by now. She had Little faith in them but still lived in hope one agent would come along one day and figure it all out.

One afternoon there was a knock at the door, it was a mousy haired man holding two black bags and had on a ID he was rushing t to let him in saying he was the council on gaining entry he took off his boots seeing she had and commented on her new carpets, he carried on up the loft with no ladder this aroused suspicion so she went into the bedroom to listen as she had nothing up in the loft for fear of spiders, so nothing to take up there. He shouted down can he have a glass of water she ran down then turned and ran back up immediately suspecting something was amiss. She caught the man in her wardrobe trying to break into her safe. Now a week before Bea had commented on seeing the safe when Tabitha was showing her a dress in her wardrobe she got a glimpse of it and asked directly did she have savings to which she replied no, just passports and jewellery. She guessed this was enough for psycho Bea to try and get to it, she was relentless. Nothing was going to stop her. She called within the hr to check up if she had any suspicions Bea would listen intently and let a little yelp or grunt of emotions again, this didn't happen often she was flatlined in emotions 99% of the time from the drugs prescribed.

She needed mental health to step in but by this apparent it was clear her parents were just as messed up as she was. Stories soon sworned round town how her father was once accused of drugging and raping a young girl who went to school with Bea..oh' she had no chance of being or living a normal life this was clear.

One rainy afternoon Bea called out the blue to go for a coffee in the local cafe. On arrival she told Tabitha to stand back while she wished to chat privately about her Jesus flyers she handed out. She handed over a leaflet she had explained these leaflets were from her church group she was in to help her recover from drugs and drink. Thinking nothing of it she stayed back. They were seated down and the waitress came to speak to her alone when Bea had gone to the bathroom.. She asked is that woman your social worker? No, and laughed. She's just someone I know from school. The waitress looked confused, mentioning be careful love, she's not right in the head and that's all the info she had. But T knew this. Bea then came back to the table and asked what she was saying to the waitress like she was obsessed with all the conventions she ever had as well. Rea then hastily got up and walked over to the waitress Tabitha overheard Rea telling her firmly she was in fact Tabithas social worker and that Tabitha had lied, this was the point she began to really wean Rea out as it had gone too far, but unbeknown to her this was nothing to what was about to come.

Whenever Tabitha met with Bea should have more and more black outs thinking usually she could handle her drink and had a strong stomach. Usually it would affect her in a way she couldn't sleep as the sugars would buzz her up and that was the effect it had on her. But only when she drank with Bea she would pass out or wake with no memory at all. This kept happening. One night she saw Bea place something in her drink so she pretended to spill it at this point there would be a reaction of emotion from Bea would become quite angry to this which was odd for her to have emotions. Another red flag ! Bea became braver and braver to the point even meeting for coffee or a bite of lunch would end up in tTabitha having a black out the next day.

Bea stayed the night on the odd occasion and one night Tabitha woke with Bea standing over her holding all her childrens phones in her hands ranting some strange words which made no sense at all, Tabitha sat up asking her what the hell are you doing woman? She let herself into her house in the middle of the night and this became so unsettling. Bea reacted "oh i'm having an episode sorry", so Tabitha told her to go and felt very uneasy about her. As often as Tabitha would try to avoid her she would just turn up and demand her time. Tabitha had not figured it out at this time that all the dark happenings were Bea. She would abstain from her as much as she possibly could from there on.

CHAPTER NINE

As you know Bea has a habit or as the police call it a pattern. She would call first was the main clue. This particular day she called and asked "where are your kids are with you or your mums?" she just came out with it, she didn't approach a conversion with hi its me, she just went right to the question so keeping up with her train of thought was alarming you never knew what she was planning but knew it was imminent that day most of the time.

With Her episodes she made brash decisions of criminal intent. Tabitha replied "at mums why?" Bea said "are they safe with her and gave an alarming grunt of a laugh." Something felt very wrong T's instincts was to get in her car and race to her mother's house 20 min drive but she went as fast she could. Her four children were there, on her arrival there was a large built over weight scruffy looking man adjusting his trousers at the front door it appeared his big belly made them loose. Her mother was sitting on the stairs she seemed drowsy. But she her injection would often make her this way at first as she was unwell. As she walked along the path the man turned to leave, passing her he pushed her shoulder saying i'm going to get you Tabitha.-"How'd you know my name?"............. he just smiled creepily. Erh he was vile looking over weight unwashed by the looks of him. He made Shrek look handsome. She turned as he was laughing as he said this, she didn't take it seriously, he left closing the gate behind him. Tabitha thought she was there in time incase Bea was coming. She had no idea she would send a man to do her dirty work because of all the memory loss she was suffering. She walked in asking where the kids were. She found them all asleep, two upstairs and two on the sofa, in an unusual position. The baby had her nappy laying on her back, the boy on his front with his trousers loose. She went up to get the older boy and girl who were asleep on the bed. She called them to get them up, though they seemed drowsy. She presumed they were up late and tired napping but this was unusual for her. She knew her children only slept when they were ill during the day or just the toddler sometimes but most of the time like her full of energy. But she didnt suspect as she knew her mother was a loving Nanny who only spoiled them.

She carried the smaller children to the car and the older two climbed in the back. The oldest boy said to his sister tell mummy what that man did to you and nanny, her bottom lip curled and she said no her eyes rolled, then closed they both went to sleep. Tabitha said wake up tell me they at this point began to laugh so she thought they were fine and carried on getting the toddler strapped into her seat and they were just tired. At this point the mother ran from the stairs to the phone and called someone but this was short. Maybe the person wasn't answering or on their way down. Tabitha went into the living room where there were 6 cartons of orange juice scattered on the coffee table. She wondered where did they come from as it didn't buy this type of drink as the sugar was too high and her children already bounced off the walls so sugar was a big no no to them unless a treat once a week of a chocolate during their shop they always had a treat on a trip to Tesco at weekends. She knew her mother didn't buy them so presumed it was her aunt who took them down perhaps. This wasn't the case.

Tabitha seeing the drinks and it being a hot day took a sip from one that seemed part full. She then left and headed home on the long drive.

Upon driving the children home Two miles was all she managed when she began to feel her eyes going and she couldn't see or keep herself awake. She tried to slam on the breaks but she blacked out at the wheel. Unsure of how long they were all unconscious she Woke up on the bank opposite the local garden centre gates. The engine was revving the doors locked as she woke she panicked all the kids were dead she feared but asleep, she screamed is everyone ok anyone hurt? They all opened their eyes saying ok mum,this relieved her. She heard a bang on the window it was the man who just at her mums house. He was being aggressive saying I'm going to get you smiling. He tried with no avail to open her door. Another man pulled up in his car and shouted `` ok mate, I've called the police ``They're on their way." At this the big man turned and ran to his car saying you're very lucky love. On this note Tabitha put her car into gear and got out of there fast..off home she went windows open to keep herself alert. She didn't think to call the police on the man she couldn't think straight, more worried it would look like knowing her luck she would have been nicked for crashing as the police have been known to get everything wrong a lot.

She arrived home and took all the children into the house. Suddenly they all had serious stomach cramps and headaches. She couldn't think straight and felt very dizzy so she locked the house up and bolted the doors from inside as her house keys had gone missing the last time Bea had visited. She wished she had called for a Dr. It's easy to see now in hindsight but her head was spinning and she was always told if you have the flu stay away from the drs. So how could she get help there wasn't any.

They all went to bed to sleep it off. T couldn't think or remember much about what was actually happening to her to even ring for help or make sense of anything but sleep. A hr went by and there was some banging at her door. She went to the window looking down, it was the big man with 6 cartons of orange juice under his arm. Held in a tea towel. He said "come down love I won't hurt you I just want to talk" she replied no we all have flu sorry, he then turned nasty shouted i'll get you as he turned heel and left. In that moment Bea phoned whats going on any news she asked, this was no coincidence she knew what had just happened, but T was drugged along with her children and mother all with something that affected their memory a date rape perhaps/GHB who knows she doesnt know what they use only by what shes seen in films.

Tabitha mum realised 1 she wasnt raped, she insisted her and the grandkids were all raped by a big man. Nobody listened to her, the drs even said her symptoms were of a fever and labeled her without visiting her as pneumonia. Her sister stayed with her the week she went down to 5 stone and waited for her die. This was what was decided. During this period there was a carton of orange juice left she was fed this as she was too weak to lift her arm to feed herself, so her sister gave it, she perked up for five minutes and shouted it's drugged, it's drugged, the orange is drugged. The sister insisted she was hallucinating there is no man here.

Bea called Tabitha and asked how her mother was doing even saying oh well if she died at least a loss is a loss never mind; she was saying cold things then blamed it on her episodes. Tabitha hung up and couldn't be bothered with Reas mental illness that day.

Bea had gotten away with something dark but it wasnt apparent or surfacing due to memory loss from all being drugged by whatever was in the orange juice he clearly had a link to Bea, he clearly had this crime down as successful and had definately done this before he was experienced therefore Bea had found someone to do her dirty work at the right price her money she was rolling in had found her a serious candidate but not a wise one just a braun dumb man who left incimiation clues behind. Evidence wasn't thin on the ground but the police needed more details, they needed it in layman's terms to solve this crime, but do they ?~ surely there is an agent who can figure this out !! . I think there is hope.

A Couple years had gone by, Bea had stayed away but it wasn't long before her fix was needed to heal her inner demons and the only way she got her kicks was to hurt others. This sunny afternoon Tabitha was sitting at home with her children playing in the yard, Bea called and asked her where she was and what she was doing. Nothing T answered,so she popped round for a quick cuppa. This was a coffee Rea insisted on making the coffee, but Tabitha walked in on her catching her throwing something into the coffee jug, it appeared to look like sand. So Tabitha washed out the jug and started again, this angered Bea for some odd reason, she wasn't happy, why was she reacting to this it wasn't her house or her coffee it hadn't cost her, {red flag}….and had to make a call pop out and meet someone quickly in the street in their car collect something and came back in this was odd secretive behaviour, she refused to tell what she was handed as well. T suspected Rea was back on the drugs. T said she had a headache and hinted for her to go. She was acting odd again and this didn't sit comfortable having her around her kids, she made her nervous but her mental episodes in the past where she's pulled knives on her toddlers and her was a scary thought in the back of her mind. T felt like whenever she tried to get rid of Rea she would become psychotic and so felt she didn't want to risk her pulling a knife in an episode again. So Rea insisted she help by getting T some pain killers so she went to the kitchen to get some, but Tabitha sneaked in peaked over her shoulder catching Rea shoving some brown powder into the capsule there was white powder in the bin, she'd evidently emptied a normal pain killer and filled it with a drug. But it felt like she'd already let her guard down on the first coffee earlier that perhaps had already been drugged; it was way too late to react now. She told Bea to leave and she did, this was a big relief.

Just after bea had left. A knock at the door her neighbour came and said hey Tabitha do you fancy a glass of wine? as he pulls a big bottle from his coat and laughs, now he was a good friend, a single parent like herself they got on like best friends and so she welcomed him in. a short time later two unsavoury men appeared at the front door and the neighbour answered it, these two men were suddenly aggressive and clearly wanted to do some harm to Tabitha she didn't recognise at first through blurry eyes but one of the men was the big man who had already attacked her mother and children. They were very agitated their plan failed as bea was to drug them all and they were to come to attack them all but this fell through. So she thought.

Early hrs of the morning came and Tabitha was awoken by Bea and two men standing over her bed, bea was pointing to T demading they rape her. She was like I'm paying you to do what I ask now. Tabitha blacked out. Bea had stolen the keys to the house that's how she had gained entry. Tabitha had no memory of this due to being unconscious.- But the flashbacks later it all came back clear as day of the moments she was semiconscious.

It was clear every time she would meet Bea bad things came along with it, but this memory loss was affecting her in a massive way.

Let-there-be-justice....................!

It was the summer holidays, the children were about to go back to school for their new year, new uniforms growing up, enjoying the last bit of the summer at home. Bea had called inquisitive to what T was up to that day, where she was and was she alone the questions usually end up in some form of darkness. T had a baby, a toddler, a small boy, a little girl, and the eldest teenage boy all of which are still in school. Within minutes of ending the call the Bea, there was a knock at the door but before she could get up from the sofa the big man had walked right into the house. He acted friendly and said I'm a friend of Bea. She sent me here to say hello. T replied eerrrr.. Ok… and immediately text her friend a plea of help to help get rid of this man who'd just arrived. The man was acting nice, handed out orange juice cartons to everyone, it being a hot day with no suspicions. (because she had no memories _) her gut instinct was rattled and danger felt. He even squirted some juice on the floor for the dog. This made her mad she shouted don't do that dont give dogs juice and you made a mess now please leave she shouted. He grabbed her phone from her hand violently saying "who have you called .?". He demanded her to open it . At this moment he had a call come in on his folding black old fashioned phone, which was clearly a throw away device to use to contact Bea. Tabitha heard Beas voice and knew she had set up this attack as he said to her don't worry I like a challenge. I'll do this now, he bragged.

Tabitha tried to run out the house to get help but she felt herself collapse and being lifted up. (her neighbour later said she saw Tabitha being carried unconscious) this was a memory jogger to help later down the line.

He placed Tabitha down in her living room standing up right she didn't know what was happening the drug had taken its toll. She turned to look at him and he pushed her down onto the stone floor violently. Before she could speak he kicked her in the left cheek cracking her upper jaw (she later found out from a dentist x-ray.) He then followed with a right hook knocking her out.

She woke up with him slapping her saying wake you need to suffer, I was paid to do this look, he waved £1000 in her face bragging Beas name and her fathers name included in the plan, he was dropping names in confidence she would not remember anyway. Or to pass blame to save him taking it all. He stood up, went outside and moments later came in throwing a black duffle bag on the floor in the middle of the living room. As he dropped it she could hear tools clunking. He said while unzipping the bag, smiling the entire time his eyes glazed like Beas, something dark, no soul behind them. He said I've been told to take an eyeball, but that's a bit gross as he grimaced, he turned away looking back and swung in down on one knee he pulled pliers trying to open her mouth as he said i'm going to take a tooth as proof. She clenched her jaw and he couldn't open her mouth, this angered him so he punched her out cold again.

She woke with his fingers in her mouth and he was laughing saying "let me get that tooth", she bit him as hard as she could not letting go. He cried out in paint let go, let go you bitch but she didn't, she left her teeth marks in his hand. Then another punch came down upon her. Out she was again. She awoke from her dogs crying in pain in the next room, she called out to them, one of them came through the hatch the other 3 couldn't jump as high, she came through stood guard and attacked the man, ripping his calf open deeply. This angered him. He went to his bag and pulled out a large knife, he went into the lion's den the kitchen full of 3 staffys, and one puppy, but he even tried his best to bite him all of the dogs ripping into his legs in self defence as he was beating them slashing them with his knife, one came through tabitha laying on the floor unable to move or scream for help. Paraylised.

The dogs cried in pain and fear he was smashing all the appliances up to shouting bet this cost a lot, bet this cost a lot,and kicked the washing machine in, kicked in the tv screen, broke the table, let off and beat the dogs with it. He said well that ones dead he kicked one puppy across the room. He bounced off the cooker and laid stiff knocked out. Then he turned to the oldest one saying;"is this one your favourite?" as he jumped up and down on her until she took her last breath bragging she was dead, she wasn't dead but a broken rib (according to the x ray at the vets) as he was getting pleasure from slashing all their snouts he took the pliers to one and pulled one of her back teeth out the cries of the dogs pain was ear piercing (the neighbour made a complaint about the dogs and t was forced to rehome them because her dogs were noisy) injustice they saved their lives almost giving thiers to save the children.

The man came back into the room, she asked him what is your name, why are you doing this? He said you can call me swifty! Tabitha had heard that name from someone else he was well known in the area for {raping dogs} sick deluded individual the police let slip through their fingers due to his many many victims suffer memory loss. He had done a stretch inside for it. If this was who Bea liked to mix with, no wonder they were as sick as each other both loved hurting kids. She had previously asked Tabitha did she have any baby cameras in the house monitors or cctv out the blue she rang to ask this almost like she was getting on indirect threats/hints, she wanted to be recognised for her crimes and plans, she wanted to be feared but she had to pay others to do it. This gives her pride and a feeling of power.

He came back into the living room standing over Tabitha with a large kitchen knife, one of the dogs stood between them snarling and growling protecting her, he came forward and span her round grabbed her tail and threw her across the wall into the wall. She tried to get a grip but slipping on the shiny floor he chased after her upstairs she ran and jumped on one of Tabitha young girls in her bed, she called out to the dog, she'd thought the dog had cut her but the big man had stabbed her in her bed trying to stab the dog he stabbed the little girl in her foot. She cried mummy mummy mummy help mummy her cry was enough to get Tabitha the strength off the floor and up the stairs but her oldest son had already made it to her faster, he had stopped the man who was raping the little girl he shouted get on your knees bitch and whale of cold scream of pain come from her. Her older brother shouted get off my sister you sick fuck get out you fucking prick sick pervert shes a child, the man shouted don't be a hero kid laughing and hit the boy to the floor dragging him back to his room bashing his head into the upper part of the metal bunk bed, where his little brother was unconscious from being drugged by him to keep witnessing eyes from what he was about to do to thier mother. A carefully planned sick attack.

He twisted the foot round on the boy until he heard and felt it crack he broke the boys foot(he couldn't play football for weeks for pain)

The man next turned his attack on the younger boy who suffered autism, learning disabilities so he hated being touched. He had his routine and everyone was used to assisting his needs. The man dragged him up slapped him awake and pulled down both the boys trousers and poked them with his hand they shouted get off you fucking gay. They kicked and fought as much as they could but nobody had the strength to fight him off even if they weren't drugged he was too strong. The little boy ran to the loo, locked himself in and the man bashed the door in half down the middle, then dragging the boy by his arm and throwing him back in his bed. Bea had carefully made sure the children's phones were all stolen a few days before on her visit they happened to go missing, this was planned, they later appeared a few days after the attack. She made sure there was no way of calling the police.

T had got herself up crawling to the top of the stairs he ran past her now I'm going to hurt the two babies ok laughing as he ran round her. He pulled the toddler from the cot she was in with the baby for some odd reason, don't know who put them to bed,but he grabbed her in her sleep threw her across the entire room she bounced off the radiator breaking her arm (x ray and cast given in hospital) he went round picked her up and threw her again. She stayed unconscious for a moment. Tabitha was screaming for him to stop but she was unable produce the sound, he then punched the baby in the cot in the face misshaping her skull (midwife commented on her black eye and head shape) he then laughed said i'll break her leg, and he dislocated her leg at the knee. She screamed and passed out. Tabitha ran at him she couldn't get her body to listen to her demands she wasn't able to cry out but somehow she ran and pushed him off the baby backwards he went. He grabbed her by the throat and pushing her backwards with one arm he said bitch you're about to die, her toddler got up off the floor with a broken arm she was hitting him trying to push him off shouting get off my mummy, he then kicked her backwards into the wall her head hit the skirting board and she looked up in pain her mother shouted " stay back "stay back holding her arm out to back away to safely. He pushed it out the landing and pushed her down the stairs, she felt herself tumble and hit her head.

She woke up at the bottom of the stairs unable to feel her legs from the ribs down, unable to move her legs but she could move her arms but her body was too heavy to push herself up. She was facing the wall sitting on the right cheek in an upright position. The man was standing over her "i'm not finished with you yet" as he dragged her up she said my backs broke. I can't feel my legs, get an ambulance he laughed I don't care"I've been paid to kill you all tonight." As he dragged her up there was a loud grinding sound three times then a massive crack and she passed out in pain. She woke up on the living room floor he was raping her. She said stop, he said im raping you bitch and pulled her hair hard and punching her violenttly. She grabbed hold of one of the testicles in both hands with all her strength. She twisted them round twice, digging her nails in hard and pulled as hard as she could, but this only angered him more and he knocked her out again. Just before, She managed to give him one good kick but he took the knife to her foot rubbing it up and down to skin the top of her foot, he then twisted it all the way around until her ankle and her fibula was broken. You're very flexible he said laughing as he got pleasure from the bone popping sound.

CHAPTER TEN

She awoke again. He was standing by the door. He laughed again and said I'm going to give your dogs and kids another bashing. I'm going to have some fun with them running out the room. She tried to scream and lift herself up to go save her kids. She could hear their screams.

He came back in handed her the phone hed taken off her the afternoon before holding her and her children hostage all night until the next morning torturing them all the entire time. In a mental frenzie. He handed her the phone demanding she unlocked it. He knew she had texted someone and wanted to delete all the msgs to make her not have any evidence or reminders. She took the phone and distracted him she called 999 and slid the phone under the sofa, it got through he lifted the sofa up in the air looking for it said what have u done.? He took the phone and either lied to them or he hung up and was pretending she doesnt know. But he told her she was very lucky, he kept calling her love, as he peeked through the curtains to the road he said the police are here now so I can't kill the kids tonight, I was told to kill them and set you up for it as he laughed about this plan. His story kept changing; it was apparent he wasn't very bright. If he was in America he would most definitely be on death row by now.

He then went up and carried the boys one under each arm unconscious, threw them onto the stone floor and standing on their backs piled them up on each other stomping on them with his heavy gerth they awoke crying in pain. He said you got to watch this bitch. He took out a hammer from his bag and said if you don't let me take photos and smile for me i'm going to smash your toddlers brains all up the wall with this hammer, he said i'll then take the baby from the cot smash her through the glass window into the garden bellow, think about the mess it will make of her face when it goes through the glass. He was smiling the entire time his eyes were blue, cold and empty, nothing was behind the eyes he was soulless, like the devil had already taken it away.

Next he went to the toddler her arm already broken he dragged her down and started to peel back her big toe nail. She screamed in agony and panting in fear he slapped her round her little face, told her to shut up and kept hitting her . She was trying to wake her mother from unconsciousness. She could slightly hear and make out what was going on but couldn't find the strength to get up or move. He laid all the children on the floor and took photos, he said they want photos as proof of what I do for them. He was using her phone sending photos to them and using his disposable phone to also communicate to them about the progress.

He slapped Tabitha, woke her up, sat her up and took photos. He stripped her down and dressed her up in someone else's skirt for the photo. She had worn jeans that day so didn't know whose clothes she had on. He went to a seriously mentlly sick level on this carefully planned out heinous act.

He held it by the face firmly and placed his flip black phone to her ear she heard him saying its ok just say it now, as he placed the call to her ear Bea said now you're going to watch your children die so you know what it feels like to feel a loss. Tabitha asked…" why?" and he hung up and knocked her out one more time.

She managed to crawl to the window and place her hand flat on the glass but was unable to shout. Someone was parked outside and perhaps sitting in making sure nobody desturbed her. A second man black hair short, ran in the front door and asked where he is, she pointed up stairs, she thought he was to help but he was- in -on- it. He ran upstairs and unleashed a beating on the children; the two men had them screaming in fear.

He ran back down by this time T had found a mobile phone and said shes called the police she told them to leave now!!!. The smaller man with violent force took the phone and cut her palm where he grabbed it so fiercely. Smashing it to the floor and stamping onit. The second man tried to hide his face Tabitha said I've seen your faces l will identify you it angered the smaller man looked at swifty, he laughed said she won't remember anything tomorrow, he had great faith his drugs work he was clearly in practice of this, She wondered how many other victims are out there being kept silent ? Evidence wasn't thin on the ground.

The smaller man said, I've just driven three and half hours to do this. Why didn't you wait? He replied just hit her. He didn't want him witnessing what he did to the kids. That's why another witness he perhaps didn't trust, perhaps that's who needs to be grilled for information, he could -be the key ! The smaller man knocked her out and she woke up being dragged into the living room from the hallway.

They were both standing over her the big man offered the little guy to rape her if he wished, she was in and out of unconcounses so doesnt know if he did. The smaller man ordered the other to knee cap her. So he pulled her right leg straight and pushed with his palm her knee cap round to the outside, he then pulled his hammer and two nails and hammered him into her knee.

He flipped her over and nailed one nail failing with the first attempt and then managed to get one into the flesh. The second man stamped on her jaw breaking both sides (dentist confirmed this) the big man decided to dislocate her finger just for fun.

CHAPTER ELEVEN

The next morning she woke up on the cold tile floor. She'd been sick in her sleep, her head pounding. She felt pain everywhere but was still out of it very much. She looked at her finger, and just decided to get hold of it and do a quick sharp straighten it and it popped back into place with a sharp prolonged pain. She felt her knee out of place; she knew she had to get leg straight to fix it; she'd seen enough football injuries, so she just pushed her leg out and it popped back in. next she reached round pulling all the small nails. Her back was bloody with a round under the skin red bruise. It was agony but worse to not get it over with and fix it. Whatever he drugged her with was acting as a painkiller, she was still extremely disoriented.

Her children came in, stood over her in a daze and walked back out delirious. She was still finding it hard to wake up. The man was still in the house..everything spinning all from a soft drink….. I don't think so… they were still in Imminent danger.

Swifty stood in the living room, collected his black duffle bag and took it to his car. He had taken the baby growth off her baby and used it to wrap around his own injury from the dog ripping his leg. He was bleeding very badly. He said now you've been had she might leave you alone, Tabitha said fuck off get out..! She wasn't afraid of him, he may be stronger but that's all he had going for him.. Not a human being but an animal, ~~~no, animals are better. He walked over to her as she was still unable to get up off the floor and stood on her left forearm until it went pop. "there you go haha" she.......said "you know what, you piece of shit neanderthal!" He turned and said don't even think about calling the police cus I will come back and make you watch me slit your kids throats one by one and he left laughing.

As he got in his car that was parked outside the house he shouted back that's it lock the door love before I come back in and fuck you up evn more this time I'll kill you.

She noticed a trail of heavy blood all the way from his car from his leg to her kitchen floor where there were puddles of blood and it was splattered all the way up the wall.

At that moment Bea called it was 7am," why ru calling me?" She said you called me last night, no I didnt the man had my phone all night, she said "you remember ?" she began to be psychotic again so Tabitha hung up. She called back to hang up. And she kept trying she msg saying i'm coming over now. In a threatening way.

Her children then came down the stairs, the older daughter said mum I had a horrible nightmare I was being raped and conor saved me, the man went to stab the dog and stabbed me and look my foot, she lifted her foot and there was a stab hole. Her pj's were ripped at the side and her bed was covered in blood. So were all the dogs. One looked dead. He had stiff legs in the air and wouldn't wake up. But eventually he did. The daughter said mum it's ok it was a dream. The dogs must have had a fight. I must have kicked the bar on the bed and cut my foot. Everyone went into Logical though as our memories faded from the night before like a switch had been flipped. ~nothing!

The toddler came down and said mummy pointing at her mouth said man hurt me. Tabitha handed her a warm bottle of milk and she asked was it a bad dream she nodded. Tabitha was perplexed at what was going on and they all had nightmares.

She went up to see the boys one had a black eye the other his foot was all bloody and grazed the man had held his foot and rubbing a knife up and down toe to ankle skinning his entire front of his foot. He said mum I cant move and I'm really ill. I think I have flu again. He then as quick as he spoke his eyes rolled up. She thought he had the flu so she went downstairs to bring him some water and a cold flannel for his forehead. On making sure he was comfy she went to check the baby. She found her lips were blue, she quickly picked her up and blew into her mouth and her eyes became wide open and she let out an almighty scream. She had a black eye and a swollen face on one side. She looked and tried to straighten her leg. It was stuck dislocated. Tabitha quickly pulled it straight, it popped back into place and the girl cried then passed out. She rubbed her leg and cuddled her until she opened her eyes, with the lack of memory nobody could remember anything they all sat together and said mum what happened last night we cant remember nore could she it was a blank and she didn't remember drinking any alcohol. It was another moment she knew she had to avoid Bea she was convinced she must of seen her the day before or something that's when it usually happens.

A couple of weeks before Bea was sitting in Tabithas kitchen with an ex who hated Tabitha he used to say he wished she died in the heat of an argument. Which happens often. She came into the room at the right moment, overheard him say to Bea;" I can get you a number but it won't be a real number it'll be a disposable phone. She said yeah do it. He said leave it with me.

That same morning, Bea arrived at the house with Tabitha's ex. She just presumed they were a couple as she used to go after Tabitha's boyfriends a lot. She was infatuated with her and wanted to be her and the jealous ran dangerously deep. Each time Bea had organised a attack she would pop to see or call Tabitha the next day like she got some sick kick from it she couldnt help herself like a murder always goes back to the scene of the crime and she was heading rapidy to becoming a serial killer if she isn't stopped soon.

She handed Tabitha a beer, of course it was laced again. She was topping her up to make sure she would heal and not remember to tell the police, and it's clear now the ex was in on it. Tabitha started to say how she got her black eye. It was the man. That's all she could remember. One snippet but the drug kicking in Bea had spiked her with. Rea looked up at her ex and said oh she remembers they both looked at each other with deep concern.

He grabbed the beer away and began to tip it he said i'm saving you, Bea came into the room and forcefully took it from him and handed it to T demanding she drink it . The ex looked silent with concern like he was too deep in it but seemed to want to back out now. But Bea was calling the shots she had got herself to the top of the chain in the gangs and drugs.

She established herself as a violent villan a independent twisted minded sick woman who needed mental help before she really does get away with murder.

So on the big sleep, it seemed to work the blood was washed away her kitchen was bleached clean Bea had done her evidence polish the finger prints and dispose of the orange juice cartons and to pry Tabitha for info she may remember and carry on drugging her for a few days while her injuries healed enough to not ring alarm bells in memory's eye. ~It was Articulated to the extreme that saving herself was REA covering her tracks.

Now it's clear who was doing it all, and who was causing the black outs. On the night Tabitha went home with Jonny the movie star, on two occasions, Bea had asked where was going that night, and Tabitha told her, the big man was in the bar that night and it was him who managed to spike her drinks intending to follow her and attack her but with luck it was Jonny who took her home, this is why she had the black outs with him, she was spiked. It was the same big man who attempted to break into Tabithas house the night jonny was sleeping in her bed, johnny was her witness they watched him from the window. It was the big man who punched Tabitha another occasion jonny was a witness. It was the big man who jonny warned her about at the club one night he told her not to go to the loo alone he's not right in the head warned johnny. ~Johnny is a witness!

All witnesses have been named to the police, all the other clues line up the man may have had to go to the hospital to get a dog bite seen to tennis and stitches, perhaps there is a record?

What do you think ?

CHAPTER TWELVE

So let's go back to the beginning just a quick recap;- the flashbacks began because the big man followed Tabitha home one night talking to Bea and she ordered him to follow her. On doing so he stood outside her house watching in for about 20 min the people in the house all witnessed him standing there staring up at the windows. He was creepy but nobody knew him.

Another day, Rea called to ask her a random odd question: do you leave your door open for the dog? She found this alarming and walked down the stairs. At that moment there was the big man lunging at her dog with a screwdriver. She asked him what ru doing in my garden. He posed as a workman telling her he was there to do the wall that had fallen, Rea knew it had repairs booked. This was a perfect excuse. She stepped out the back to see a ladder he had climbed in because her garden gate had been locked up. On the ground were 6 cartons of orange juice. She pointed to them; they looked old and manky like they were years out of date. He must have these stashed ready for when he needs to attack someone using the same old trick will slip him up one day,- it's a pattern!

He left shortly; he was just doing a trial run to see if he could gain entry via the back. A short time after Tabitha had taken photos of this man and his truck with the ladders it was a flatbed he had gone to a lot of trouble to drive round drop off his ladder along the wall and go park the truck in the car park in town. To later be used to gain entry to her home.

This was a new address some years had passed from the last attack but Bea was addicted to them at this stage getting more and more involved herself now. She arrived out the blue one day demanding she take Tabitha including her 15 year old daughter at this time she was grown up baring in mind this mans already raped her twice since she was 9 and 12 ish, now 15 Bea has set it up again.

She took them both to a local cafe. All they drank was a pot of tea and a coffee. Bea said close your eyes don't open them I have a surprise . she popped the lids of the teapots and said ta da here it is enjoyable. I hope you both like it. Before they knew it they were all over the place and couldn't see or walk like they were drunk. Feeling high and sleepy. Bea perks up" lets get you home ". Tabitha said no we're not going home but Bea got nasty grabbed hold of them and dragged them back . Bea was being unusually aggressive; she was determined to get the girls where she could set her dog upon them, her new best friend swifty. As soon as they arrived into the house Rea walked into the teenage girls room and opened her ground floor window. Tabitha caught her, demanding her to close it and get out of her room and walked her to the door, making her leave. Rea sneaked back into the house, but abitha caught her forcing the locked handle and breaking it so it wouldn't lock, making the excuse she thought it needed air. Tabitha made her leave and got mad at this point, getting out now and locking the door behind her.

She went back into the room to close the window and caught Swifty . He'd just climbed inside. He ran at her and knocked her out, as she tried to run along the hall away from him. She woke up on the sofa he had dragged her up and placed her out the way. She could here her daughter cries she went down to see her and he was there raping her, she was screamin for him to stop no no, Tabitha shouted get off her and ran to call the police but again he grabbed her and smashed her unconcious into the door frame.

After being unconscious for god knows how long it was The next morning, she went down to see her daughter, having woken up with a black out. There were orange juice cartons next to her bed, and she had a huge black eye. Tabitha asked did you have a big man in there last night or did I dream about it? She replied "mum, don't say that I've been having these nightmares again the same as I used to have as a child. " She refused to tell any more about them. Tabitha asked how did you get the black eye? I don't know, I must've banged it on the bed in my sleep. She insisted she must have the flu and wanted to be left to sleep. (evidence; the window was reported to the housing for repairs it needed a new handle and they found a screwdriver pry mark on the outside)

Few weeks later, Bea called and arranged a family meal with her family. She insisted she go but she's not allowed to drive herself. So she went along to let them collect her, the meal seemed nice but she caught Beas sister throwing some brown powder onto her dinner. She suspected she was already drugged. She was starting to figure things out at this stage and realised she was being spiked around her.

She thought quickly and went outside, called 999. On arrival the police were no help. They arrested Bea, but left her to cope with falling unconscious with no ambulance even though she begged for help the police said no. On that note Beas' entire family laid into her outside and beat her up leaving her on the side of the road near her house. The sister even tried to plant the drug wrapper in her bag telling the police but Tabitha suddenly realised it was apparent and said" yes fingerprints it'll have their fingerprints on it," in that moment Bea had been stood there listening and panicked didn't think this well grabbed the wrapped away in fear of her finger prints and making herself look guilty she was handcuffed.

Another occasion Bea had posted under a fake acc ohotos of Tabitha on line just after she was raped, naked unconcious she tagged her in and over 250 comments saying rape call the police, but still evidnece is thin on the ground.

In the light of day.......

The Trigger to the flashbacks... the big man Swifty he calls himself, decided to go knock on the victims door after Bea had called him and told him Tabitha had taken a photo of him walking from her garden, he walked back to the house knocking the door, standing with one arm up high leaning against the glass looking down as she peered up at him, he said in a threatening manner " do you know who I am?" she replied no, " well keep it that way," he turns to walk away, pauses, turns his head and follows with "if you know what's good for you. "!..............

It was at this exact time she realised there was something familiar about this man's eyes she felt she had something else to remember. This is where the flashbacks began and why they began, he triggered them, it was his own downfall, ~*he should have stayed away*..........!

All The Prison Guards In England ~Await Their Company.

<u>The End</u>

Lightning Source UK Ltd.
Milton Keynes UK
UKHW010648050422
401078UK00001B/9